GEMETERY ROAD

SCRIPTOR HOUSE
The Epitome of Greatness

POOKIE MARCEAUX

Scriptor House LLC

2810 N Church St Wilmington, Delaware, 19802

www.scriptorhouse.com

Phone: +1302-205-2043

Published by Scriptor House LLC

Paperback ISBN: 979-8-88692-192-2

eBook ISBN: 979-8-88692-193-9

Contents

1

Imagine a place where ladies are not ladies, but what some might call animals, trapped in a small cage, never knowing if it's night or day.

Chairs were flying; ladies were disobeying orders and pushing each other, crashing to the floor with no remorse.

Once again crazies were disobeying orders and wouldn't settle down for their daily routine, a routine that consisted of heavy medication so that no assistance was needed.

They could do nothing to help their own self and became unable to communicate with anyone.

They pulled their hair and shouted weird sayings.

It was a normal Friday at Sunny Side State Mental Institution.

Or was it Friday?

Sunny Side was established in 1898 and located near the swamps of Aster, Louisiana. A small populated community known as Cajun land. Many older Cajuns lived on houseboats surviving off the wildlife and what the land had to offer. They refused to go or live near the institution. The nearest town was eleven miles away, separated by a dilapidated bridge crossing over the bayou. The bayou was filled with trout lines and crawfish traps. It was surrounded by rice fields and oil wells. Gravel roads and wood frame houses described their way of living.

Sunny Side earned respect caring for the insane. New arrivals were welcomed if you dare allowed one of your love ones to be checked in.

The hospital resembled a three-story English cathedral surrounded by giant oak trees. Large concrete columns were wrapped with Spanish moss.

Doors were made of steel and windows were covered with barbed wire. It was poorly kept and appeared to be haunted. Tall weeds had taken over the flower beds. A wooden porch swing hung from the ceiling by rusty old chains. Shutters were hanging by on hinge and slamming against the outside wall.

It was nearly impossible to escape and those caught were severely punished. If you escaped the facility, you may not get out of the swamps alive. It was filled with poison from the black cottonmouth. You can't let the noise of the swamp control your mind. Giant cypress trees nearly reached the sky. The swamp was also home for coons and the golden owl. Large alligator snapping turtles ate a persons leg in one bite.

If one was caught trying to escape, residents were placed into darkness and left there for days with no food or water.

Residents were placed on one of three floors according to the seriousness of behavior and illness.

Their conditions are so horrible and hopeless as far as having any better life….this place was filled with fear.

The first floor of the asylum was divided into three large rooms separated by thin paper walls. It was very cold and patients were not allowed to wear socks. The only means of heat was the sun shining through the windows.

The cafeteria; It didn't have the aroma of appetizing food being prepared.

It was infested with insects and grease covered equipment. Rat and roach droppings lay throughout the kitchen area. Floors were covered with filth. Mealy bugs crawled out of every box of cereal or oatmeal. Stoves and ovens were not set at the right temperature and most of the food was not properly cooked.

Cooks were ordered to use dirty utensils hoping the resident would become ill. They never wore head caps and hair folic lay atop the residents plate. Residents were forced to eat everything that was served. If someone became sick, they lay quietly in their vomit.

Ladies were slumped over in their chairs trying to hold on for another day. Their faces lay helplessly in a plate of food, while others stared hopelessly into space. Some laughed aloud, while others yelled weird sayings.

Dried beans one day, rice the next. Stale bread and a cup of water were considered part of the daily menu. Orange juice was not orange, but brown. Spoiled rice had a taste of it's own, not to mention a few dead roaches which was to be considered as protein. A container of warm spoiled milk was drunk from a dirty glass. Figs injected with castor oil was desert. Devil eggs smelled rotten. Lettuce was black and tea was sour. These items were placed on a tray in front of them. If they chose not to eat, then it became a personal problem. What the residents didn't eat, roaches and flies enjoyed.

The game room; Dim, dreary, large and very cold. A table, deck of cards, and a checker set with several missing pieces lay on the floor in the corner. Some imagined the lights of Vegas, while others never realized cards were missing from the deck. They laughed and joked and for a moment life flowed through their veins. A puzzle with three missing pieces was considered finished. A globe of the world was rarely looked at and was caked with dust.

The so-called sunroom had little or no sun. Most of the windows were covered with tin foil. It was okay for those ladies who tanned daily. They only needed ten minutes to feel young again. Lotion was not allowed because nurses feared residents would drink the poisonous liquid. If the resident gets burnt they must suffer or heal the best way they know. A vinegar bath in hot water was offered, but rarely accepted. Some were tossed in cold salt water and left for an hour or more.

The second floor was a mystery. No one talked about all the rumors concerning this place called the dead zone. Residents believed it separated echoes of pain between the first floor and the third floor.

The third floor being the worst was so frightening with lunatics that many employees refused to work there. The old walls creaked as you walked down the corridor.

No doubt, the crazy one was watching you.

Every step taken was possibly your last.

You could trust no one, and no one trusted you. There were only eight residents who were severely mistreated.

On one side of the room, sits Eleanor blankly starring out the bar covered window all awhile thinking, "across that fence is my family and their waiting for me. I must keep looking so I don't miss them, she thought. If I can't get a ride I'll have to walk home in the rainy stormy weather." Eleanor was a small lady who needed hip surgery. She could barely walk and needed a wheel chair to get around.

Mary stood in the corner having been forced to keep her nose in a circle drawn on the wall. She appeared to be in a world of her own as she stood there for twelve hours, never realizing the meaning of time. Her feet were swollen and she could hardly walk. All of a sudden she clapped her hands three times and laughed out loud. Mary was quiet at times and caused no trouble. All she wanted was the comics from the daily news. She read and laughed a loud, but no one listened.

In the center of the room, Velma, an older woman sat on the floor continuously brushing her long grey hair. Velma muttered to herself as she counted the strokes. She rarely took a shower, but washed her hair daily. A miracle was bestowed upon her, no tangles. At times she would stand near the window so her hair would glisten in the sunlight.

Jennifer rocked back and forth talking to her imaginary baby that was covered with an old dirty blanket. She sang lullabies of unknown origin with heart and soul as if her baby was alive in her arms. She rocked for hours while others waited for their turn to rock-a-bye baby. She threatened to cut to Velma's hair off if she went to sleep.

Brenda was a known gambler who carried three decks of cards in her rear pockets and poker chips filled her front pockets. Many cards were missing but she insisted on having a quick game. Once being a wealthy young lady, Brenda wasted millions at the casino. She knew the game, but forgot her name, which caused her to go insane. She shouted aloud, "my jack can beat your ace."

Connie was labeled trailer trash and no one cared. She came from a poor family who lived below poverty level and survived on prayers. She was skinny, about ninety pounds with knurly hair and rotten teeth. Her weight dwindled due to food infested with bugs she couldn't chew. She wore oversized clothing and resembled a rag doll. No family members visited as she sat alone near the window with no hope for any life.

Margie tried getting other residents to understand the severity of the freezing cold air that filled the room. She wore a heavy coat, old thermal socks, three pair of sweat pants and a quilted hat. Although the temperature outside was a heated 98 degrees, Margie continued to cry out loud----"it's cold in here, please turn up the heat." She sat alone on the end of the stained sofa hoping someone would listen. She had a touch of Down syndrome and was probably admitted into the wrong sort of facility. She had a weight problem and took a bath at least once a month. An imaginary odor filled the room.

Some were aged, while others showed their youth.

Some talked in tongues and believed the head administrator was the lord and they would be set free.

The administrator was never seen and at times you might wonder if he ever existed. His daughter was ill and all he was concerned about was her well-being and not the sickness that was widespread throughout the asylum.

He relied on his secretary to carry his workload. He gave most responsibilities to nurses and guards. His view towards the residents was cold and hard.

He treated them like a contagious disease. Veterinarians took better care of their dogs with distemper.

Long nights at her bedside and watching her slowly fade away, he asked why.

"Why are you taking this lovely child and allowing those lunatics to have life?"

"It is unfair."

Well, fairness is never used to aid the residents. Nurses pulled residents by their ears leading them to their rooms. A moan or cry out load was not excepted. That only led to a cruel and unusual punishment. This one rule the administrator did not conjure up.

Nurses forced the residents to kneel on rice on a concrete floor with their nose in a circle. For one hour they were humiliated and forgotten.

The administrator would never find out because he gave little care to his job, a job he maintained for thirty-eight years. He made all the rules and his way was the only way.

No need to complain, cry, etc., it was not open for discussion.

He took pity on no one and stood tall against the insane women who challenged him.

It mattered not, because they had no life. Hope remained for those who were young. Many were young, but their minds were old.

They knew one place, one home; the *asylum,* a place where disturbed minds drifted beyond the strawberry fields.

Some residents crawled around on the floor, while others sat there, laughing in amusement. Many were simply unattended, while others were in a zombie like state of mind.

Echoes of fright could be heard, as inmates cried from fear of pain.

The smell of urine filled the halls. It was a smell from *hell* that brought tears to your eyes. Hours would become days as helpless residents waited for the housekeeping department to clean the sour smell that was nearly unbearable.

Infections from wounds left unattended began to seep a thick yellow fluid onto the floor. Bandages and ointment were denied in hopes the residents symptoms would worsen. Swelling and fever were part of the pain.

Residents tried to cope with unknown illnesses.

It made no difference to the staff if someone complained.

This was an insane asylum different from any other you have heard about. No one seemed concerned about the health of women trapped in a world of their own.

Not only were these ladies lost with reality, but were mean and very insane. Nurses were told, when hired, you should never turn your back on a patient. A fifty-fifty chance was all you could hope for.

There was no room for error, as non-licensed nurses were specially trained to overpower residents who might cause them harm with physical violence. It was impossible to hire good registered nurses because of the dangers involved.

Straight jackets and two inhumane tactics scared only a few, neither of which you nor I would feel comfortable with.

Stage one: A large needle injection caused severe pain and the out of control resident slept 48 hours. Eyes filled with tears as blood dripped down her arm. A burning sensation caused her arm to swell. A loud cry, a moan, a whimper and the patient slipped into silence.

Stage two: They were forced to stay in a small 8 foot by 8 foot padded room. Nurses used all means available to overtake the uncooperative patient. It was cold, dark and very quiet, except for the sounds of crazies. They were left alone four or five days without food or water and were stripped to the flesh and not allowed blankets or pillows. A cot and a toilet were all that was available. If you did not have enough energy to get to the cot, one lay helplessly on the cold, hard, concrete floor. Medication was overlooked and the residents unstable and weird symptoms seem to worsen. Night after night and no sleep for many, except for the chosen few who were injected with a thick serum. Some say it is made with a small amount of rat poison, honey, and sea salt.

Echoes of pain bounced off walls as residents cried out loud.

No one cared and no one listened.

Rule #1: Never stare into the eyes of the insane. You could get trapped into the confused mind of a person who could overtake your mind and also your actions.

I suppose what was once a beautiful woman, did not comb her hair for months and has dark circles around her blue eyes. She wore a torn dress and her feet were caked with dirt. She was allowed to shower every ten days, but did not understand how it could rain without any lightning or thunder. She talked rapidly and no one understood her. She walked backwards, but talked in circles.

This resident, Darlene U. McFarland, was a diagnosed paranoid schizophrenic. She comes from a family that is very mentally disturbed. She must be considered extremely dangerous, as she holds a record for the abusive attacks on nurses, guards, and other patients at the facility. She pounced on her victim like a wildcat, scratching and clawing drawing blood and leaving scars.

Darlene will make every known effort to escape, like a spider uses his web to lure its victim. She is insane, but remarkably intelligent and could cause great danger to others. She suffers from psychotic delusions.

At a young age she was an honor student and was accepted at Harvard University. She grew up in a social atmosphere and had anything and everything. It's hard to imagine how someone with that lifestyle would end up in a place like this.

Her hobbies were somewhat strange. She collected pottery and flower petals. She chewed gum and saved the wrappers to make a paper chain. Her favorite color was red and spent a large amount of money on shoes. She was very popular and a natural beauty with everything to live for. She was a fabulous singer and a teenage drama queen. She lived life at its fullest. Darlene was rich.

Cheerleader, Prom Queen and Most Likely to Succeed were only a few of her accomplishments before she was struck with a mental disease she could not overcome.

A perfect sane mind had gone to waste.

She can't remember her name and many people think she murdered her father, Oscar McFarland, a wealthy real-estate broker and owner of a limousine service.

He was an important member of society and Chairman of the Board for several major companies. His family has a long history in the corporate world of business. He enjoyed hunting, fishing, and playing golf. His dream was to move out to the country some day. He was a trusted man in the community, who donated time and money. Oscar was a member of the local church and participated in all activities. He never informed anyone of the medication he was taking and reports revealed he visited a psychiatric ward twice a month. These visits, for whatever reasons were unknown. Maybe it was for his own well-being and not to visit someone there.

However; his body was never discovered and no evidence was ever found. At this moment, it is pure speculation that foul play was involved in his disappearance.

Anyone who has information on the whereabouts of this person, please contact the local police in Aster.

After a large reward and time passed, no leads were reported and Oscar McFarland was declared missing and dead.

A shock to the community and to the family and friends he had touched.

It must be stated, Darlene is the daughter of the well-known wealthy investor Tuesday McFarland.

She is a widow who lives in a high-rise apartment near the city limits of Aster. The entry, surrounded by huge oak trees, had a gold gate that welcomed friends.

Million dollar investments and CEO meetings was a drop in the bucket of her daily responsibilities.

Airplane flights to every major city allowed her no time for her personal life.

She burned the candles at both ends, working all day, but finding time to dance all night. Wild parties, drugs, and alcohol of the social world controlled her. A new jaguar, yacht, and tons of money attracted the sort of attention she did not need.

Her career took precedence over anything else, including her daughter and the lost of her husband.

Big city lights and fast lane living caused her much stress. When she had a break from her hectic schedule, she came home to the small community of Aster where she didn't fit in with the lower class of people.

Many doctor appointments showed she was losing touch with reality. Visit after visit Tuesday had her doctor totally confused. She had a different story about some weird happening every session she attended.

Doctors could no longer prescribe proper medication Tuesday needed and requested she see a psychiatrist.

Like most doctors in that field of medicine, the more knowledge one had about the patient's life and history, the better they can help.

During one session she made a statement, "It's so nice to have my daughter living with me. I have a room upstairs where she stays. I feed her, read to her and take extra good care of her. I know she is very ill and as her mother I must protect her. Tonight I'm going to read her a story."

We knew about Tuesday's daughter, but she never mentioned anything about a mental hospital she was locked up in.

As days passed Tuesday seem to have more and more problems. She attended a religious service every Sunday, but could not relate to friends and people from the church.

They began to gossip, "she is just as crazy as her daughter Darlene."

Tuesday eventually quit all outside activities, stating the illness of her daughter had worsened and she must stay home for her.

Doctors have become worried because she has not shown up for any of her appointments.

"She called our office to explain," added the doctor.

She said, "taking care of her daughter who lives upstairs is the most important duty at this time."

She never mentions any other members of her family and no one knows whatever became of her husband, Oscar McFarland. She tells us what she makes up and that's all we know.

One doctor said, "we now have big trouble."

"We can't force her to see us without discussing the truth about Darlene." "She's not aware that her daughter is an escapee from the asylum and many are searching for her. "What kind of damage will we cause if she learns the truth?"

Concern began to grow because bi-polar was becoming schizophrenia to a well known lady in our society. When she spoke, people listened.

Doctors then learned about another member of the McFarland family.

While going through the files of Tuesday McFarland, they discovered the name Thomas, her son.

The youngest, of two children, Thomas was a loner.

He lived in an old abandoned farmhouse at the end of a long dark country road five miles outside of Aster. This was an inheritance from an unknown family member.

A cemetery sets across from the farmhouse which overshadows the view of an incredible swamplands. Giant cypress trees lined each side of the road. The cool breeze flowing through the treetops overpowered the summer heat. Fallen giant oak trees provided fire wood.

The farmhouse was old and spooky.

Thomas had little or no money for exterior repairs. Rotten wood barely held the front porch together. Walls were cracked, the roof leaked and several windows were broken. Paint peeled off the walls as dullness set in. Plumbing was a problem that was never discussed.

He survived with an outdoor restroom and water from an untreated underground well. Water was yellow and smelled like rotten eggs. It was something you had to adjust your taste buds to. Branches lay on the rooftop, while gutters were filled with leaves. Screens were torn and most of the wooden fence had fallen to the ground.

Thomas did not have many of the luxuries life offers us today. There was neither television nor telephone. He hoped that someday he could afford a radio.

After sundown light came from a full moon or candlelight. A bright moon was the natural way, but things were creepy and somewhat bizarre around the farm on those nights.

It was easier to see the shadows!!!

During the day the attic was hot and dusty, and at night, it was cold and dark.

Noises were heard only silence could bring. Chains rattled the windows and sheep could be heard beneath the house. You could hear shutters slamming against the outside walls.

Spider webs held the rafters together.

A small window was located on the north side of a dormer protruding from the roof.

"Someone's watching you!!!"

The interior was livable, but could use help. It was a bit small, but it was home for Thomas.

The stairway cracked with each step and the loose rails could collapse at any moment. Under the stairway a small trap door appeared to be jammed or locked for some unknown reason. There was no key around. The trap door was covered with a small decorative rug that was stuck to the wooden oak floor. It had gone unnoticed for years until one day a strong rainstorm caused water to flow into the house. Thomas noticed water dripping towards the small door. He removed the rug, pried the door open and discovered a cold dark cellar. He slowly worked his way downward with a bit of nervousness.

Spider webs hung from the ceiling and the squeaking mice quickly drew his attention. A large cot and a couple bottles of aged wine were set off in the corner. There were several large boxes filled with old items, seemingly of great value. Musty smelling clothing and other garments reminded him of his grandmother. He then found pictures of hospital rooms inside a folder. Receipts and all sorts of legal papers pertaining to the mental illness of Mary I. McFarland were found. A journal was hidden under an old blanket.

As he read on he was struck with eerie feelings. A page or two led him to believe he may have other family ties. He suddenly felt the presence of some one dear to him. Could this be his grandmother? He put the book down in awe! This was enough for now and he removed himself from this hidden room.

People continued to laugh and talk amongst themselves about the farmhouse being haunted and how some crazies live there.

Because all attention was focused on his sister Darlene, he had no friends from the city.

Townspeople refused to travel this road in fear of a flat tire or breakdown. No one wanted to be stranded after dark on *"Cemetery Road."*

Rumor says you might get lost in the fog.

Not much was known about Thomas, except, like his mother he attended local church on Sundays. He didn't have any extra money, but always donated five dollars.

He knew little or nothing about his parents because he and his sister were given up at a young age. They had their career, Thomas and his sister had that disease. He was a bit out of level. His hope one day was to find out about the life he didn't have.

Thomas, a mallard duck farmer paid no attention to townspeople and their way of living. Strange as it may seem, it was an honest living and he found peace within himself raising ducks.

I suppose he had several hundred pair floating around the man made ponds covered with dark green lily pads and red white tipped lilies. Their beautiful shiny green heads sparkled in the sun as they awaited darkness for a place to rest. A real nature spot for the average hunter. An unbelievable dream paradise.

He kept to himself and talked to only a few. He trusted no one and felt they would rob you blind, chew you up, and spit you out like gum. They're ruthless and have no feelings.

He visited the pharmacy once a week to fill prescriptions, do his business and head home. Traffic made him nervous for there were no highways in the fields around the farm.

People stared and laughed as he slowly drove down the road.

"There goes the crazy one," replied an elder gentleman.

They continued to talk and laugh amongst themselves. They joked about the farm Thomas had and how it was old and rundown. They gossiped about his job and his way of life. It was a small town and that's all they had to do.

"He's a quack," they added.

It was not all sadness around the farm.

Thomas had Slim, an old bearded farmhand who lives in the huge barn behind the farmhouse. He stood tall and had a mean look, but age had settled in. A few broken teeth and lots of wrinkles was a reminder of this. He may be old, but he is wise. He had no children that he knew of and could not speak about his family. He had no drivers license and became a hermit absorbed in his farm life. He never drank alcohol and had nothing to do with cigarettes. He was fairly healthy for his age and was under no medication. He was an honest man and Thomas trusted him. The only problem, he can't remember things. It's that disease. He slept in a hammock under an oak tree on summer nights. He tended to his daily work like he has done for twenty-years.

Twenty-years on the same old farm and little has changed. Not much is expected out of Slim; cook breakfast, help with the ducks and watch over Thomas. Occasionally he mumbled to himself, but was just like a shadow.

Every two weeks Thomas met with Reno, from the State Game Warden Department. Reno was in charge of purchasing and treated Thomas fairly for many years.

Thomas sold approximately eighty ducks at ten dollars per pair along with a friendly handshake each time. This was his life, his business.

Reno complimented Thomas again and again for a spectacular job on breeding and caring for several thousand beautiful healthy ducks. They would be released in the wild in hopes of saving a part of nature.

Thomas told Slim, "I hate to depart from our avian friends we raised and cared for."

"Well, I must be on my way, said Reno.

Darkness is setting in and I don't like it out here. I saw some old lady walking around in her yard and she looked sorta creepy.

What about that cemetery, he asked?

Thomas thanked Slim for a good job and looked forward for their next visitor.

No longer said, and a cloud of dust appeared.

The mailman's usual visits, or a weekly delivery from Albert, the milkman, were the only visitors from town.

"Good afternoon, said Albert. I'm a little behind schedule today so I don't have much time to chat."

Upon occasion he would stay for a glass of tea. It was quiet refreshing after a dusty ride.

Albert filled his order and asked Thomas if he was okay.

"Well it gets a bit lonely sometimes being in a place stuck in the middle of nowhere," said Thomas.

"Oh, I guess I could talk to Slim, but he'll forget by the end of the week."

"Time moves slowly, but we make the best of it."

"The nights are long and dark," said Thomas.

Albert accepted what he has seen around the farm and treated Thomas like a regular customer.

"Well, I'm headed to my next spot so I'll leave a gallon of milk and a gallon of juice, just like always," said Albert.

"See you next week." He leaves with a friendly gesture and a tip of the hat.

2

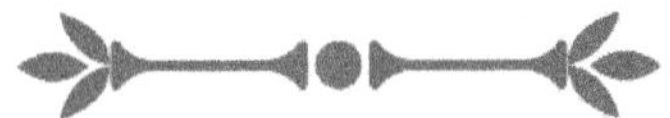

At the edge of the woods lives Isabelle, an old insane woman. It would be minutes and Albert would come to his next stop.

Albert made her a part of his weekly route, but thought she was a bit weird. Being somewhat scared, Albert was not ready for trust amongst the two, so he kept his distance and did his job.

I must say, "she wore old clothes, but she smells good." Must be some expensive perfume, he thought. She wore red tennis shoes with white leggings that looked the color of chocolate milk. When she decided to dress up, she wore a denim skirt, purple striped blouse with LSU Tigers on the back and an old straw hat.

He commented on her beautiful landscaped yard filled with kitsch and wildflowers. Blackberry and grapevines covered the fence line. Bird houses were filled with purple martins and cedar waxwings. Red cardinals perched themselves along the edge of water fountains. Hummingbirds gathered by the hundreds sucking on the red nectar from the long neck bottles hanging from the red bottle brush bushes. Blue jays and red robins were eating wild birdseed from the yard.

Albert would tip his hat, say a nice gesture, and proceed on his way.

Every time I said goodbye, she offered me a slice of gum.

Isabelle was born in south Louisiana near the banks of the bayous filled with poisonous snakes and large snapping turtles. Injected venom from a cottonmouth could cause death.

She lived a poor life and rarely had necessities. Money had no meaning and she never celebrated holidays. Every month members from the church brought over several boxes of commodities. Boxes contained powdered milk, peanut butter, beans, etc.

A normal family would find this embarrassing, but this was living like a queen for Isabelle.

A nearby sugar cane plantation allowed her to work at a young age.

She had a choice, work or school. Little or no education would lead to a glum future.

She worked from sun up to sun down walking five miles a day earning wages below poverty level.

Hobbies included collecting baby turtles, checking trout lines and killing snakes.

Killing snakes had a strange twist. She collected their heads and pretended to cast spells on those she feared or did not like.

She chewed tobacco and believed the juice was voodoo venom. She spit in a can and saved it to rub on the head of the dead snake.

She has family that was never discussed and no one from the city visits her. Rumor has it that somewhere she has a twin sister whom she fed her fruit from a poisonous tree.

Not much is known about her because no one has seen this person. They say she walked into the swamp one day and never came back. A person can not survive in the swamp after the sun goes down. Strange noises will drive you insane or the alligators will eat you alive.

No evidence of her sister's survival is known.

A spell may have been cast on her, but we may never know the truth. This could become a powerful tool if someone needed control.

Her parents believed it was another alligator having lunch and never pursued a search of the swamp.

The authorities were never contacted. Isabelle has been alone for the last thirty years.

No one was allowed in her bedroom, which was filled with evil looking gadgets. Black painted walls and lighted candles surrounded the centerpiece, a skeleton that resembled a human skull.

No maintenance so it appeared to be haunted.

Set in her way, she only accepts things on her terms.

She asked nothing of anyone and visited Thomas and Slim on a regular basis.

Thomas found a true friend and looked forward to their visits. He accepted a woman who mumbled and rambled on and believed she was a normal person. A strange feeling from an old lady he didn't know that well.

3

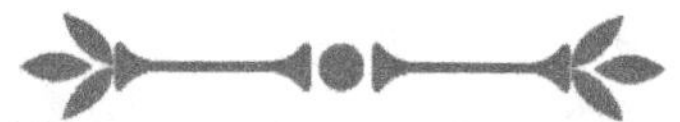

Meanwhile; back at Sunny Side Mental Hospital things continued to be out of hand, as Darlene was nowhere to be found.

Panic settled in, as staff members discussed their next move.

All residents were locked up for head count and security.

Patient's yelled and screamed with fear.

Nurses searched every room, closet and grounds, and still, nothing.

Armed guards and staff members searched for hours before noticing a medical bag with numerous bottles of medication were taken.

Several syringes that contained a sleep serum were also missing. Improper use of these drugs could cause severe damage, if not death.

Three days have passed and still no sign of Darlene.

Rumor has it; she had escaped the facility without a clue of her whereabouts.

Authorities were beginning to believe the possibility of an escaped lunatic could now be reality.

Authorities have now contacted Darlene's mother to advise her of the possible escape of her daughter from the mental hospital and the threat of danger to the public.

We told her this is a serious matter and something must be done.

We can't afford for the public to get wind of this and cause panic throughout the city.

Tuesday insisted she was taking good care of Darlene for months.

"She lives upstairs and seems to be getting much better," she said.

She invited authorities over for a cup of tea so they could visit with Darlene and witness her improvements.

4

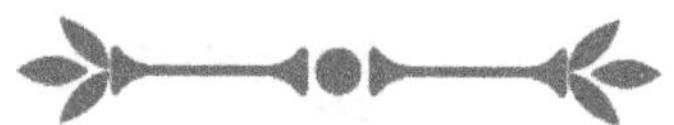

Back at the farm, the sun had risen beginning a new day. A rooster could be heard but not seen as he appeared to be lost in the morning fog. Morning dew dripped from the rooftop onto the smoke filled ground.

It was early morning and things needed to be done.

Slim had collected eggs and tended to breakfast. He made a fresh pot of coffee and was ready to begin his duties.

The smell of bacon and hot biscuits did not interrupt the thoughts flowing through the mind of Thomas.

It's been two long weeks and today was an important day for Thomas and Slim. All time and effort put forth was about to bring personal rewards.

Reno was coming today to purchase more ducks.

Thomas was excited and looked forward to this opportunity to choose the prettiest mallards to be set free; free as the wind blowing through the tops of giant cypress trees.

Slim seemed to be excited, but for reasons not pertaining to selling ducks. He appeared a bit nervous, biting his nails and pacing back and forth. I must find a way to tell Thomas, he thought.

At that moment Thomas noticed a change in Slims' behavior.

"What's the matter, asked Thomas. Are you that anxious to see Reno?"

"Thomas I must tell you something," announced Slim.

"Well, speak up," said Thomas.

"Quit your muttering and talk."

Slim went straight to the point not knowing how Thomas would react.

"While I was hunting eggs this morning I found footprints behind the barn."

"Footprints," asked Thomas.

They probably belong to Isabelle," he replied.

"She hasn't been around in a few days and those seemed to be fresh prints," added Slim.

Slim said, "we collect two dozen eggs daily, and today we were several short."

Whispering to himself, maybe it's the heat.

For now the day was hot and moving quickly. Afternoon was upon us and Thomas felt great. He had a good attitude and was ready to meet with Reno.

It would only be minutes and Thomas could see dust down the country road headed towards the farm.

A smile on his face meant the purchase of more ducks was near.

As the vehicle approached the farm, Thomas did not recognize the stranger driving a different color truck.

As the truck came to a stop, someone stepped out and said, "hello my name is Steve and I work for the Aster Wildlife Department. I'm the new purchasing agent."

"Sorry to say, but Reno was transferred to another division so I am here to purchase ducks for the department."

"I will get straight to the point," said Steve.

"Things in our department have changed. Times are changing. New technology has given us ways to produce offspring faster and very efficient."

"We no longer have the need to purchase ducks from farmers. I can offer you five dollars per pair."

"Five-dollars per pair," shouted Slim.

"I know I'm only a farmhand, but that's unfair prices."

"We should not except his offer," yelped Slim.

As Thomas pondered through his head the unfair ways of this deal he had no choice but to accept the offer.

Suddenly an offer made a smile become a sad face.

To make matters worst, Steve purchased sixty ducks instead of the usual eighty.

Slim gently loaded these incredible looking birds into the back of the truck, while Thomas stood in silence under the shade tree.

"Well, I'll see you in a month," said Steve.

"A month," asked Slim.

"Yeh, we must change our routine a little, so I'll drop in once a month."

Not much was said as Steve drove away, driving down that dusty country road with contract in hand and a smile on his face.

It was not the kind of day Thomas expected and Slim could feel his pain.

As evening rolled in things were quiet around the farm.

Quietness ended soon as Isabelle walked over and knocked on the door.

"Come on in," said Thomas.

Isabelle was asking questions about things she usually doesn't care about. She asked, "who's that visitor, I've never seen him before."

"Not much to talk about," said Slim.

"He didn't treat us right and I don't know how we will make it," said Thomas.

Isabelle appeared to be nervous or upset and talked about a shadow she had seen in the woods, along with footprints near the swamp.

"It's just a fisherman, replied Slim.

"It's that headless horseman," Thomas said jokingly.

"I'm serious, she said. Sometimes I see a glare in the woods at night. I have found footprints near my blackberry gardens. You should keep an eye out."

Isabelle new the atmosphere around the farm was rather bleak and decided that a short visit would be enough for today. She didn't stay very long and headed down that long country road towards her house. It was getting late and that meant dark.

As she walked on she became scared, scared over silence. It was quiet and spooky.

It felt as though someone was watching.

Suddenly, a rabbit jumped into her path. She was shaken up and feeling the jitters. As she looked around she thought she saw a shadow near the corner of her house. She got a little closer and it had disappeared. She ran inside and locked her doors and windows.

It would be some time before she could fall asleep and wondered what would become of the shadow.

She worried about Thomas as though he was family.

Days passed and Thomas seemed concerned about the farm. It appeared there wasn't much he could do and reality must be considered. He was quiet but insisted they move ahead with their plan for the duck farm.

Imagine an egg, a baby duckling and then a shiny green headed mallard.

"Today, you must not think about the farm," said Slim.

"It is Sunday and you must attend weekly church service. It will do you good to sing in the choir and collect money for the offering."

Thomas was polite, but shy, and mostly kept to himself. They trusted him and today could see the troubled look in his eyes and tried to find something else to gossip about.

Perhaps today will be filled with prayer, not talk. It wasn't as bad as he thought. It was a peaceful outing.

5

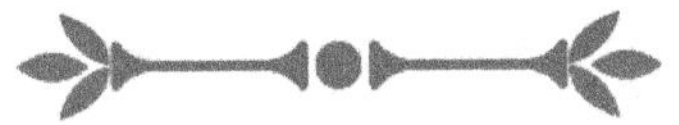

Meanwhile, two weeks have passed and still no sign of Darlene.

The mental hospital has called off all searches around the facility for the missing insane woman. There were no remains of her body floating along the banks of the swamp.

A picture of her still hangs on the bulletin board at the city post office. A large reward has been offered, but nothing to report at this moment.

"We must not let our guard down," said authorities.

"We still remain hopeful she will be found.

There are many leads, but still no Darlene."

As for her mother, Tuesday stays cooped-up in her high rise apartment. She has her groceries delivered and pays her bills on-line. Some of her close friends from church check on her periodically. She insists she is okay and informs them that Darlene has her good days and bad days. Music is the only thing that seems to calm her, she whispered. Her eating habits could be better, but I will never scold her for not eating properly. She takes all her supplements and eats her fruit.

She may be caring for Darlene, but her thoughts were now being filled with memories of her son Thomas.

I wish I would hear from him once in awhile. I miss him dearly.

I suppose no news is good news, she thought.

I could pay him a visit, but I can't leave Darlene alone. It can be frightful being alone.

Back at the farm, dust from the country road was a warning someone was coming. It was okay, because it was the milkman making his weekly delivery.

A couple of containers were all Thomas could afford this week for money was tight.

Thomas invited Albert in for a cup of tea as they were becoming better acquainted.

"I can't stay long," said Albert.

"Days are getting shorter and out here in this creepy country, that means we have more hours of darkness to be concerned with and I have several more deliveries to make before my day is done."

"Before I go, I must warn you of an escaped mental patient from the city hospital. They searched every inch around the facility, but found nothing."

"Reports say, she is very dangerous and everyone should be on guard. She could appear anywhere."

"Authorities don't have a clue."

"I believe they are scared," he said.

He added, "I'm pretty sure they said her name was Darlene"

Thomas suddenly felt a large lump in his throat.

Standing nearby, Slim overheard the conversation between Albert and Thomas.

This was not good news and at that point Slim blurted out, "I have seen her shadow in the window of the attic and found footprints throughout the woods. They could be hers. Strange things have been happening around the farm and I can't find and explanation for them, said Slim."

"You know, I think you're imagining things again, by the way, did you remember to take your medication today, asked Thomas?

Slim didn't take medication.

Way back in Thomas' mind was a thought, a scary thought.

Could this escaped woman be his mentally disturbed sister that everyone fears?

He nervously began to wonder could this explain all the noises he had been hearing in the cellar, and what about the missing eggs?

"I must leave now, said Albert. It's getting late and Isabelle is waiting. I hope I didn't scare you with the news, and remember I'll see you guys next week."

He gave a good farewell to Albert and there was no doubt, Albert left the farm noticing a worried look on the face of Thomas.

As he drove away he could see the sun setting behind the huge cypress trees and grey clouds. The nights were longer and a storm was brewing in the distance.

"Looks like we're in for a rough night," said Slim.

Slim preferred to sleep inside tonight protecting himself from the approaching vigorous weather.

"I'll keep an eye on things," he said.

He hung his head as he headed to the old barn.

It seemed like minutes and a killer storm came barreling across the farmland. Winds were howling, lighting cracked and the thunder roared. The sky lit up from reflections of a great electrical storm.

Thomas had several candles lit as he expected a long night of severe weather. He sat alone near the fireplace hearing creaking walls and mysterious noises.

Lightning struck again, and a shadow could be seen outside the window. Thomas walked towards the window and peeped outside. There it was; pure darkness.

Thunder roared and noises were heard inside the attic.

For a moment, there was silence. He could feel the presence of someone near. He knew there was talk about the farm being haunted, but could not imagine anything like a ghost being around.

Suddenly, someone knocked on the door.

"It's me," said Slim.

"I wanted to check on you because I thought I seen a shadow near the edge of the barn."

"No, it wasn't me, I've been sitting here and I think I've seen it also," said Thomas.

"Well, it could be Isabelle, said Slim. I know she gets a little scared during bad weather. I will talk to her in the morning."

Thomas muttered, we must adjust to what has happened. It is going to be a long, hard winter.

The rain began to fall as the storm continued on its path.

Slim visited for an hour or so having tea and discussing the upcoming winter season.

The mallard farm produced minimal business last fall due to the migration of all other ducks and Slim knew that would put extra weight on the shoulders of Thomas.

Bright colored male wood ducks and blue-winged teal have invaded the mallard zone. They flew in by the thousands invading the swamplands. They were looking for a place to call home but, it was getting that time of the year and it wouldn't be long before hunters would walk through the woods and shotgun blasts would be heard for miles.

Thomas had no use for hunters, for every shot fired and every duck killed could be one he and Slim had raised.

"Well, I suppose this is goodnight," moaned Slim.

Thomas walked Slim to the door and felt a presence he had never felt before in the twenty years of staying on the farm. He could sense someone was watching, but could see no further than his hand in front of his face.

Dark seemed to be more than a four-letter word.

"No use to stay up all night, said Slim. You must try to sleep even though there's a storm. You know what the next few weeks bring and you need your rest."

Nighttime seemed a bit short and Thomas woke up somewhat tired with very little energy.

Roosters were crowing and early morning was upon them.

The storm had swept through the night, like a witch on her broom, doing minor damage scattering debris around the farm. A few branches were broken and ditches were filled with water. A chill was felt in the air.

"Looks like we dodged another bullet," said Thomas.

He could smell bacon frying and coffee brewing and he knew Slim was ready to start his day facing the good or bad this day had to offer.

Slim knew it would be a difficult week for Thomas to handle.

It was not roosters that awakened everyone, but gunshots. Shotgun blast throughout the area sounded like World War II.

Yes, today was the first day of duck hunting season.

Rice lands, canals and marshes were filled with artillery as hunters tried to bring home the most trophies. They were ready to lay down their decoys, shoot ducks and let their dogs retrieve. Hunters took pride in who had the best trained dog. Most chose the black lab while others preferred the chocolate lab. It was a challenge deciding who the best callers were. It quickly became known as the duck capital of the world.

Shots suddenly became louder and louder.

Clutching his ears, Thomas shouted, "thank god there's a limit on the amount of ducks you can slaughter."

"I can't understand why someone would kill a harmless bird, just to mount it on his office wall," he added.

"I wonder how many walls are filled with ducks we raised," asked Thomas?

Slim shook his head for he could not say much. He felt somewhat guilty because he has two friends who were hunters.

The two hunters were young and just having fun, he thought. He knew how Thomas felt about his friends and it wasn't very pleasant. I guess he had that right. Slim knew that any moment they could arrive at the farm for their annual visit.

Not much more was said, as voices were heard at the edge of the woods.

Closer and closer, louder and louder the noises grew.

Within minutes, the loud talk and laughter were the two hunter friends of Slim. They approached the farmhouse with loaded guns and several dead ducks. Their dogs patiently walked at their side.

Slim greeted his two friends with a hug.

"Been a long time," said Slim.

"Nice to see you again," said one boy.

The two boys were very pleased with the first day hunt. They bragged about all the green-head mallards they and their friends had killed.

"There were so many ducks, it was hard for our dogs to keep up. Our buddies did better than us.

"There were ducks everywhere," they laughed.

"I've never seen many in the past as we seen today," they added.

"We killed a bunch," said one hunter."

Whispering to himself, "you mean slaughtered," replied Thomas.

"Wow, look at all those beautiful green head mallards setting on that pond over yonder."

"That's amazing," he said.

Jokingly, one hunter replied, "maybe next season, we will set out decoys and hunt right here."

"You guys have no respect for nature or what it means to preserve wildlife," said Thomas in an angry tone.

His temperature was beginning to elevate after that last statement.

This was not good, because Thomas was a very sick man and Slim was aware of his illnesses.

He could see the worried look in Thomas' eyes and was beginning to be concerned.

Slim knew winter had just began and Thomas was already settling into his winter mood.

Thomas was stricken with high blood pressure, diabetes, emphysema, and congestive heart failure. We must not forget that all his family members are mentally disturbed.

The hunters did not stay long thereafter.

"I think we should leave before darkness sets in," said one hunter.

"Yeh, I would if I were you. No one wants to be out in these woods after dark, said Slim. It can get a little spooky."

"Oh, by the way, we found a small campsite at the edge of the woods, but no one was around. It was old and run down, but we could salvage it for a weekend camp out. We found a box of matches and several bottles of aged home made wine. There was also a piece of paper, perhaps chewing gum paper lying on the ground," they said.

Slim didn't say a word, but he was now thinking about all the mysterious happenings going on.

Footprints, a shadow some missing eggs, and now a campsite that appeared to be abandoned. He knew Thomas was upset so he planned on keeping this to himself for a while.

The hunters tipped their hat to Slim and apologized for upsetting Thomas. They wandered off into the woods, talking loudly and celebrating a successful day of hunting. There was a limit on ducks but most hunters overlooked that law and brought home as many as they wanted.

Echoes could be heard in the distance.

Hunting season lasted two weeks and Slim knew it would be difficult for Thomas to deal with.

Slim walked over to the farm house with the intention of giving Thomas his view of the situation.

"I know times are rough right now, but I have this feeling things are about to change for the better," said Slim.

"We'll do the best we can and try to survive the winter," added Thomas.

7

Days seemed like weeks with little or nothing to do around the farm. It took a couple of hours to pick up the scattered debris from the storm.

It was a lonely life stuck way out there with nothing to do.

"Maybe we will see IsaBelle today," said Slim.

The day had moved slowly, but a change was taking shape.

Dust from the country road appeared from out of nowhere.

It was the mailman bringing Thomas a surprise he was not expecting.

A letter arrived and Thomas did not recognize the return address. He read it twice to make sure, but he didn't understand.

"What you got there," asked Slim.?

"Looks like a letter from a cousin I've never heard of," answered Thomas.

Thomas tore open the envelope and began to read……

Hello,

My name is Amanda Norwood. I have been waiting for this moment to discuss the possibility that I may visit you for a short period of time I realize you do not know who I am, but, I believe together we can answer a lot of questions that placed doubt in our family history. I will be arriving in two days. If you do not want me to stay, I will understand. I hope you read this letter with heart and be anxious to see me.

LOL, Amanda

The name Amanda didn't mean much to Thomas and he truly believed he had never met her. She supposedly is the niece of my father except that I didn't know my father had a sister.

"I think she wants to spend time on the farm with us hoping we can become better acquainted and take time out from big city lights," said Thomas.

"Well, I guess we should get ready, said Slim. Things are a mess around here."

"I know it's a bad time right now, said Thomas, but we'll make the best of it. We must pretend everything is okay. I want to welcome her with open arms, even though we do not know who she is."

"Maybe she works for the CIA," said Slim.

"It really doesn't matter because we'll find out in a couple of days," added Thomas.

He told Slim to make ready the room at the end of the stairs.

"It's the best we have and it's near the kitchen," he added.

"I hope those creaking noises doesn't scare her," joked Slim.

"Everything will be different here."

"It's not the big city lights and fast lane living that she's used to," said Thomas.

"It's go to bed early and get up with the roosters," replied Slim.

After twenty years Slim had never seen Thomas hurt so bad.

He knew he was a sick man and he must pray that Thomas could withstand what he was about to face.

"I must make sure I don't let him down," he thought.

Thomas began to ramble on and on, "I don't trust Steve."

"He has put us in an awkward position for the winter."

"Times are hard and money is slow."

"What will we do?"

"We won't have enough eggs if she visits for awhile."

"I suppose we could borrow some from Isabelle," joked Thomas.

"She's always ready to lend a hand," added Slim.

As they joked around, the sun was setting in the distance. Flashes of light could be seen.

8

Later in the night another ferocious winter storm hurled through the evening.

They were not prepared to wake up the next morning with debris scattered throughout the yard.

Branches were snapped and the ground was soaked.

Your bones felt pain from the immense wind.

Smoke rings from your lips drifted through the wind.

They had one more day to clean up the rubble from the storm and extra work meant less time to prepare for Amanda's arrival.

They knew it would take hours to clean up the small disaster and faced having to help Isabelle repair the damage she incurred.

"Winter is hard and I hope Amanda can handle the change. I must take care of things around the farm, I don't have time to baby sit her," said Slim.

It seemed like days had passed, but it was only hours, hours of worry and concern, not knowing what to expect.

Slim worked spending hours repairing and making sure Amanda would be comfortable with her stay.

He cleaned and cleaned until he had the white glove effect.

No spider webs for a few days would be worth the effort.

Thomas decided to take a short break before he got started. He sat back in his chair and grabbed for the daily newspaper.

Worry struck again in a serious manner.

Headlines….

"TWO HUNTERS MISSING AND PRESUMED DEAD."

Thomas read the article quietly to himself, but moaned on several occasions. He had reason to be concerned.

The next sentence read, "hunters were last seen near, "Cemetery Road."

He continued to read the article learning more about the case.

Evidence revealed articles of clothing, a shot-gun and a gum wrapper were discovered near the east-side of the cemetery. Footprints led to the edge of the swamp where a syringe was found.

Many thoughts flowed through his mind about the missing hunters.

Could they be Slims' two friends?

This was not the best of timing for Thomas.

Two hunters presumed dead and a cousin he didn't even know was about to arrive.

Should I keep this a secret, or tell Slim?

How must I keep this under wraps?

He was faced with the decision of telling Isabelle.

He began to shake and sweat dripped down his brow and he couldn't remember if he had taken his medicine today.

Thomas drifted away in his own thoughts.

9

Two days have passed and time was near for the arrival of Amanda. It wouldn't be long now and Thomas must put his patience to work. He was waiting to meet his next of kin he knew nothing about.

That thought was soon interrupted by a cloud of dust headed towards the farm. As the dust cleared a large, shiny, black car sat in the driveway.

We could see nothing inside because the windows were dark as night.

Sweating palms and a nervous Slim standing beside me, made the welcome seem uneasy.

Finally, a big, tall man stepped out and tipped his hat.

"How are you gentleman doing today," asked the driver?

"Just fine," said Thomas.

A nod from Slim meant the same.

"It's been a long, hard trip, but we made it," said the driver.

"It took several days, sleeping and eating on the road. We got lost because there were no signs leading to *"Cemetery Road."*

It's kind of spooky out here," he whispered.

"It's not a road people travel or like to talk about," said Thomas.

"I was sort of bothered," said the driver.

The owner of the service station said, "don't be caught on *"Cemetery Road"* after dark.

He then told me, talk around town had people believing that some have not returned or has never been seen again.

"It's just rumors," replied Slim.

"Well, there's a lovely lady I would like for you to meet," said the driver.

He opened the rear door and out stepped a beautiful young lady.

"Please meet Amanda," he said.

She was tall and slim with crystal blue eyes. Her long, black hair glistened in the sunlight. She was dressed in red and wore red high heels. Diamonds and necklaces covered all necessary spots.

It was like someone stepped out of a magazine.

She smiled and held out her hand.

"Hello," my name is Amanda.

"You can call me Mandy if you like."

"Hello," said Thomas, "nice to meet you."

"This is my farmhand," Slim.

A nod was all you would get out of Slim.

A beautiful long hair calico cat lay asleep in her arms.

It was hard to distinguish the beauty between the cat, or Amanda.

"I would like you to meet Daisy," she said.

"She's like a child to me. I hope it's all right to keep her around. I've had her for several years."

A small lump in Slims throat caused him to cough aloud.

"What about the ducks," he asked?

"Birds and cats aren't a good mix you know."

"I'm sure everything will be just fine," added Thomas.

Thomas had never seen anything or anyone so gorgeous in his entire life. He knew nothing about this person, except she was his cousin.

A flashback of his mother showed some resemblance to Amanda.

Slim walked around in circles lost for words.

He appeared to be very nervous as he gnawed on his fingers.

The driver unloaded all her bags of luggage along with a large trunk, but was unsure what to do with them.

"Just set them on the porch," said Thomas.

At that moment, Thomas began to worry if there was enough room for all of her belongings.

As Amanda walked towards the old frame house, Thomas could only wonder, did she expect more than she is getting?

Judging the way I see things, a city gem has now become a country dust buster, he thought.

Thomas admitted he wasn't sure what to expect upon her arrival.

"I see now we must give her the big room," he added.

"Yes," but the big room is a big mess," replied Slim.

Thomas offered the driver a glass of tea and he accepted.

They sat and visited for an hour or so and it was time to be moving on.

The driver turned towards Amanda and asked, "would you like to stay, or go?"

"I'm going to stay," said Amanda.

"I think I can make a go of it. It's beautiful around here and it will be a pleasant change."

"Beautiful ducks," announced the driver.

"Thanks," said Thomas, "it's a job like no other."

Thomas bid farewell to the driver and welcomed him back anytime.

He drove away slowly leaving behind a trail of dust.

"Well, I guess this is the beginning," said Amanda.

"You and Amanda can get acquainted this evening," stated Slim.

"I'll be here in the morning with fresh eggs for breakfast."

"Goodnight," he addressed and headed back towards the barn.

"Where's he going," asked Amanda?

"Oh, he'll be all right, he lives in the barn outback."

"In the barn," she questioned?

"I think you'll find our way of living a bit different," said Thomas.

He made it clear that it was not like society life.

"You know, money being tight we get by with the necessities."

"We have no T.V, but we make the best of it."

Amanda smiled and whispered, "please don't worry, I'll be fine."

Not lacking wit, she said, "we'll pretend we're camping."

The sun was beginning to set on the first day of Amanda's journey.

"We must figure out where we will sleep tonight," said Thomas.

"We will start a new day tomorrow, get organized and everyone will have their space."

With a tear in her eye, she gave Thomas a big hug and assured him everything was going to be all right.

"I have a deck of cards and a checker set," added Thomas.

"I know how to play chess and backgammon," she said.

"Several years ago I went to Bourbon Street in New Orleans. People were playing this game with a half a deck of cards. I think they called it "EUCHRE" (Yucca). I understood the game better than the name. I'll teach you and Slim someday."

City lights would grow dim as dark drew near.

You could fell the cold setting in.

"I'll gather some firewood," said Thomas.

"I brought a pillow, blankets and a few things to decorate my room."

"Is it okay to call it my room?"

"Of course it is."

"Our home is your home now," said Thomas.

"Tonight you can sleep in my bed and tomorrow we'll get your room together."

Not much of anything was accomplished that night.

They talked for awhile, but never mentioned family. I was hesitant about conversation hoping not to push any wrong buttons. I wasn't sure at what time we would get on that subject, she thought.

"Well, we must call it a night," said Thomas.

"We have a big day ahead of us," he stated.

"Goodnight," said Amanda.

Night seemed longer than usual and perhaps a new face would brighten things up around the farm.

10

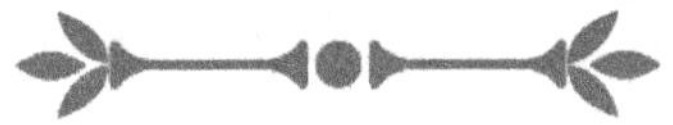

As the sun came up brightly, morning brought a special joy to the farm.

Thomas woke up ready to face a new day. He called out to Amanda, but he got no response.

"She went for a morning jog," shouted Slim.

"A jog," asked Thomas.

"I don't think she is aware of what goes on around here."

"We don't want to scare her, but I believe she needs to know and understand the dangers."

"What do we tell her exactly," asked Slim?

"Tell me what," asked Amanda as she appeared from out of no where.

Silence overcame Thomas.

He gathered his thoughts and replied, "I must tell you everything about our family and *"Cemetery Road."*

Amanda pretended like it was no biggie.

She grew up in the city where crime became the middle name of many.

She took everything with ease and believed that with enough money you could fix anything.

She refused any stress level that entered her life and was a young lady who took time to smell the roses.

Thomas recommended she tells him about her morning jogs, or late afternoon walks.

"It's important that you tell me all the details," he said.

"Details," she asked?

"It's just an old country road, what details are there?"

"Yes," said Thomas, but you must listen to the silence around you and the time you leave so I will know when to expect you back ."

"It will give you an eerie feeling like no other," said Slim.

"Perhaps the presence of someone watching you."

"Perhaps," she answered.

"It was a great jog and I didn't see or hear anything unusual."

Slim muttered, "you will."

"The morning air was great and I enjoy watching the sun rise."

They gathered around the breakfast table and began eating fresh country eggs, crispy bacon, golden biscuits and a fresh brewed pot of French roast coffee.

Thomas had no idea where to begin the conversation of family and whatever necessary things needed to be discussed.

He asked Amanda to be patient so he could gather his thoughts.

She couldn't imagine anything worse than big city hanky pranky politicians stealing your joy.

"Well, I have an idea," she announced.

"Let's go into town and do some shopping."

"I'd like to plant a rose garden, flower garden, and our own vegetable garden. That old house on the corner down the street has a beautiful yard. It's hard to overlook, so we should do the same."

Thomas stared at Slim with that honest look in his eyes.

"You know there's one small problem," whispered Thomas.

"We don't have the extra money for those items…. we can only afford the necessities."

"Okay," she responded.

"You must understand something," she said.

"I have plenty of money and we can buy anything you need or want. There will be no boundaries."

Thomas witnessed a smile on Slims' face, something he hadn't seen in years. If there was any sadness during any point of the morning, it suddenly turned to joy.

"Plenty of money," asked Slim?

"Yes," answered, Amanda.

"Lots of money."

"We should do a facelift around the farm."

"Well, if it's all right to do that," she asked?

"Many years have gone by and we never imagined a facelift."

"Where would we begin," asked Slim.

"We should do a total upgrade," added Amanda.

"We will paint, repair the roof, and lay down new flooring. We'll get electricity and all the modern things of today. We can make a list of things needed and a supply list. If we take our time and get a game plan together, I think it will be a fun project."

Thomas could not foresee such an undertaking.

He knew a trip to town would mean more explanations.

"I think we should make it another day," said Thomas.

"Today we must introduce you to Isabelle plus the milkman makes his weekly delivery today," added Thomas.

"We might not have enough money for milk," replied Slim.

"Sure we do, remember…..I have lots of money," said Amanda.

Thomas wasn't sure to what extreme Amanda was willing to go with spending her "lots of money."

He gathered they were not on a tight budget, but never had this luxury before.

There appeared to be many daily duties today, but no one was willing to get moving.

They just talked, joked, and laughed for awhile.

Smiles filled the room.

It was a memorable moment for their first morning.

"I believe she was God sent," said Thomas.

"I think we should get going so we'll have enough time to get everything done," added Slim.

"Please don't worry about time," she said.

"My time is equal to my money and I have plenty of both so let's enjoy the moments."

They walked out onto the porch and gazed into the morning sunlight. The yard was filled with red breasted robins.

"Let's walk down the road and meet Isabelle," asked Amanda.

"Okay, let's go," said Thomas.

Every step taken had meaning.

The gravel beneath their feet and dust along the way was something to make conversation about.

Every few steps, Amanda would pick up a rock or two and toss them into the woods.

"Be careful," laughed Slim, "you might hit someone."

This was no laughing matter.

Within seconds they all witnessed some sort of shadow at the edge of the clearing.

It then suddenly disappeared into the cemetery.

"What was that," asked Amanda?

"Someone was watching and no one knows who," whispered Slim.

"It could be my insane sister who has escaped from the mental hospital or my father who hasn't been seen for years," added Thomas.

"It might be Isabelle watching the new kid in town," they added.

"It could be…….

Thomas hesitated, as their journey would end sooner than expected.

A cloud of dust was racing like the wind and within seconds it was upon them.

It was Albert delivering the milk and juice.

He stopped in the middle of the road in awe.

"Hello," said Thomas.

"Hey guys," what's up?

Albert tipped his hat to the unknown lady.

"We were on our way to Isabelles' house so I can introduce her to my cousin who's staying with us for awhile," said Thomas.

"We still have a ways to go."

"She's not at home. I stopped to make a delivery and no one was around. I could feel the presence of someone, but saw nothing," said Albert.

"No telling," whispered Slim.

"Would ya'll like a ride back to the farm," asked Albert?

"Yeh," sure, that would be nice, replied Thomas, and oh, by the way, this is my cousin," Amanda.

"Hello," Amanda, very nice to meet you. We don't get many pretty girls in our neck of the woods."

I believe it was love at first sight for Albert. He had never seen such a beautiful girl before. Miss Hollywood had just arrived on his route.

"How long do you plan on staying," asked Albert?

Amanda smiled, "I'll stay here as long as they let me."

Suddenly, the cloud of dust disappeared and we were back at the farmhouse. Albert made his delivery and asked if we wanted it added to the bill.

"I suppose that's okay," said Thomas.

"It doesn't have to be that way," said Amanda.

"How much do we owe?"

Thomas put his head down in an embarrassed way not wanting Amanda to know how much debt he really is in.

He had been charging his milk and juice for months and the money owed was adding up.

"I'll say this for the last time," Amanda announced.

"Money is no object."

"I have plenty to go around."

"Now, the bill, please."

Albert handed Amanda the bill and smiled. He didn't plan on two miracles in one day.

"How about some ice tea," asked Thomas?

"Sounds great," replied Albert.

After a few minutes, Albert turned toward Amanda and said, "I'll be back next week and I'm looking forward to a pleasant visit."

"Well," I must go now. I have people waiting."

"Oh yeh," by the way?

"Did you hear that those two hunters are still missing and there's no sign of that crazy lady that escaped from the mental hospital. Probably should keep your eyes open," he added.

He walked away with a smile moving on to his next stop.

"We've been knowing Albert for a long time and we never seen him act like that before," added Slim.

"I think the love-bug has bitten him."

"Stranger things have happened," mumbled Thomas.

"What hunters, what crazy lady," asked Amanda?

"We will discuss this later," answered Thomas.

"Please don't worry," he said.

Amanda had a lot of energy to burn and she did not waste any time speaking out.

"Enough of this, she stated, "let's go uptown and shop."

"I'm ready for plants and flowers."

"We will make a change around here for the best. We will add some color to this place."

"What will the townspeople think and say," asked Slim?

Being from the city, Amanda wasn't concerned.

"Let's just go and we'll worry about that later," she added.

"I must tell you something," said Thomas.

He looked into her eyes and began talking slowly.

"Everyone in town believes we are some sort of outcasts and we don't belong here. They will laugh and tease us. They know nothing about our lives, only rumors they start."

"We try not to let it bother us, but it does."

"Okay, I understand, added Amanda, let's leave now so we can get back before dark."

"Yes indeed," replied Slim.

"The night brings out the shadows," he said.

They headed towards town with an open mind and thoughts of everything going smoothly.

As they passed Isabelles' house they noticed someone standing near the fence.

Within a flash, there stood no one.

"Why do we keep seeing people who aren't really there," asked Amanda?

"I know there are no such things as ghosts," she laughed.

"There are a lot of things on *Cemetery Road* that can't be explained."

"It sort of makes you crazy," said Slim.

11

Soon they would arrive into town just before lunch. Everyone was rushing around like a normal Saturday morning.

People were gathered like flies and had burning visions in their eyes. We only wondered what thoughts were embedded in their minds.

Someday, we may come to know and understand, thought Amanda

You could feel them stare and see their whispering lips.

Amanda knew about gossip because of big city thieves that steal your smile and taste for life. Nothing bothered her, but she could see the strain on Thomas' face as they proceeded down the street.

It was not what she expected, a single lane main street with a limited amount of stores for shopping. It was very old and rundown. A five and dime store and a drug store were the main focal points. The Post Office was combined with the bank.

It seemed no one cared about anything but themselves.

On the corner sat a small café. It took care of all menus' from a to z. There was a pool table in one corner and a pinball machine in the other. It was the city hangout for both young and old.

"Let's enjoy what the town has to offer us while we are here," said Amanda.

Thomas was amazed how she made him forget all hell the world has to offer.

Within minutes they would finally reach the only plant nursery in town.

As they got out of the car, Amanda noticed several people starring at them.

"Who's that beauty," asked a stranger?

"She must be new in town," whispered another.

"Yeah, but look who's with her."

"She's too pretty to be a member of that lunatic family," laughed another.

Whispers became talk, as people gathered around wanting to know, who's that golden beauty?

Amanda and Thomas walked around taking notice of all the greenery and bright colored flowers.

Thomas had no idea where to begin. He didn't have a green thumb, so he knew he would be no help in making decisions about choosing plants.

"She's as pretty as all those flowers," said one townsman.

They walked and walked, and Amanda bought and bought.

She purchased all sorts of flowering bushes and fragrant plants, hanging baskets and all related items. There would be no limit.

As time passed Thomas was seeing a new light. Things were taking on a new change and he felt he had no part in it.

Maybe it would be for the best.

"I must trust Slim and Amanda," he thought.

They loaded the items they had purchased and was excited about the adventure they were about to take on.

As they drove away, people were still starring.

What felt like hours for Slim; was not much time spent at all.

He seldom went into town because he knew everybody would be watching every move he made.

They knew who he was, but he knew no one.

"Not to bad," said Slim.

"I thought they would tease us a bit more than what was said."

"Probably the sight of a most beautiful stranger wilted their thinking," said Thomas.

"As we leave town, I want to show you our church. I sing in the choir every Sunday and was hoping you would join us."

Thomas didn't know that Amanda had a talent hidden deep inside her.

She could sing like a canary and no one knew.

"I would be honored," she said.

"I believe everyone should set aside a day for worship and praise."

"Are they going to whisper and talk, or will they listen," she asked?

"I will give it my best shot," she replied.

"Oh, by the way, is there a library around here?"

"I have always had an interest in becoming a writer."

"It was something I think I can do with my spare time," she replied.

"Write about *Cemetery Road,*" added Slim.

He may have chuckled, but I think he was serious, thought Amanda

"I believe I could write about *Cemetery Road*, but I will need to do some research," she added.

"You'll be able to write and write until there's no more paper once you gather information about this family and where we live," replied Slim.

"Writing about our way of living should be kept a secret."

"It's nobody's business and we must keep it that away," said Thomas.

Amanda could feel a bit of tension when talking about certain things. She was beginning to understand the feelings Thomas had about his family and his life. Yet, she never crossed the line about questions she still had no answers to. She didn't push any buttons because she knew Thomas would open up to her eventually.

Talk about becoming a writer dwindled as they departed from town.

Amanda spotted Ursula's Voo-Doo Shop on the way out.

"Let's stop in and get better acquainted," she said.

"Maybe some other day," whispered Thomas. "We should never go there unless we have run out of answers."

"Well, not a bad outing for our first trip into town, she added. I enjoyed the ride and we should do this more."

Silence filled the car for about ten minutes.

Amanda could only wonder what was going through Thomas' mind as they drove down the highway.

She was unsure of what to say next.

Out of the millions of opinions, hers was weak, thinking silence was the road to wisdom.

"Say, can you turn the radio on," asked Slim?

"It might help out the mood and we can feel the joy through the music."

"Only church music brings me joy," said Thomas.

With a smile, Amanda stated, "let's pretend we're in church!"

Songs of joy soon became songs of sadness because city life had practically deteriorated his soul and sad to say, Thomas felt he was growing old.

"Pity for dishonest people drove me out of the city," said Amanda.

"Living in a city, I thought would be a good life.

There were many good points, but mostly I noticed the bad ones.

Those who thought they were right; led others to death.

Their minds were obsessed with power, while their tongues ran like sand flowing through an hourglass."

"As we learn to accept many nasty remarks from shallow minded people, I'm sure city life means well," she added.

They were getting closer to home, which meant traveling down that long dusty road.

12

There was plenty of daylight left and that might allow some planting time when they reached the farm.

As they entered onto *Cemetery Road*, they noticed Isabelle standing near the ditch in her front yard.

Thomas slowed down because she waived her hand as though she was trying to get his attention.

He stopped the car and rolled down the window.

"What's going on," asked Thomas?

"I think there's some sort of trouble at the end of the road," said Isabelle.

"Trouble," asked Slim?

"What kind of trouble?"

Thomas could tell Isabelle looked a bit shaken.

She mumbled a few words and walked away.

They drove a little further and Slim noticed several law enforcement officers sitting in parked cars along the edge of the woods.

As they approached the area they were stopped by one of the officers.

Thomas rolled down his window and asked, "what's going on?"

"Do you live around here," asked the officer?

"Yes, sir," answered Thomas.

"We have a serious problem," stated another officer.

Thomas looked at Slim in a nervous fashion.

He didn't want Amanda to become scared, so he pretended everything was all right.

"What kind of problem," asked Thomas?

"We don't want to put fear into anyone, but we're looking for two bodies near the pond on the other side of the wooded area. It appears that they were hunting and haven't returned. We will have a lot of questions. Maybe you know something that will help us get to the bottom of this."

"Two dead bodies," replied Amanda.

"Kind of reminds me of the city life I left behind."

She seemed to take the news with ease and acted as though it didn't bother her.

Slim could tell that it bothered Thomas; he didn't take the news very well.

"I bet it's my two hunter friends," said Slim.

"They haven't been seen for awhile, so some family member reported them missing," replied the officer.

Slim put his head down, not saying another word.

"We found several pieces of evidence," said the officer.

"Do you chew gum," he asked?

Thomas looked over at Slim and answered, "no sir."

"I do," said Amanda.

"We will have to ask you some questions young lady."

"Okay," she replied.

"Need not worry," said Thomas, she just arrived a few days ago. I hardly believe she had anything to do with this."

"I noticed an elderly lady at the end of the road."

"We will talk to her about this incident also," replied the Sheriff.

"Probably won't get much out of her," added Slim.

"She's a bit off level and you will never get a straight answer."

"Do you know if she chews gum?"

"I believe she sure does," admitted Thomas.

"That will be all for now," replied the sheriff.

"If we need more information we will contact you."

"We will do a thorough investigation and find out who is responsible for this.

"Crimes like these cannot go unsolved."

"Thank you for your time and help," he added.

Thomas drove off slowly and headed towards the farm.

He seemed a bit on edge as usual and worried about what Amanda might think.

"See, I told you to write about *Cemetery Road,* we always have stuff going on out here," said Slim.

"What was that," asked Amanda?

"I think I seen someone or something in the woods. It was like the shadow we saw before. It appears that's all you ever see around here."

"Maybe I'll write a book and call it, "The Shadow.""

As they arrived back at the farm, Thomas took a long gasp of country air to clear his head.

Slim could sense something was different, so he asked Thomas if he remembered to take his medication today?

"Yes," he replied, but I don't think it does any good.

Slim and Amanda unloaded the car and gently placed the colorful flowers throughout the yard.

She tried to change the mood by asking Thomas, what was his opinion?

She could tell he was not interested by his response.

"It doesn't matter," he said, "it looks great."

"Whatever you decide, I will accept."

"I believe I will go inside for a while."

"I need to rest, I need to think," he said.

Amanda, who wanted to become a writer was suddenly lost for words. She could feel his pain.

Slim seemed less bothered and helped Amanda arrange the plants and flowers.

Deep in his mind, he knew those bodies that were missing was his two hunter buddies and could not imagine the horror they encountered.

Could this be their punishment for slaughtering our beautiful ducks all these years?

13

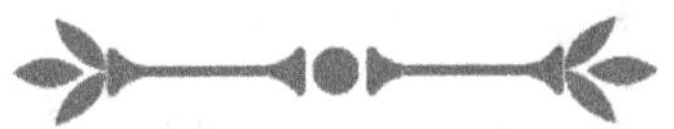

Meanwhile, Thomas was pondering over the information he had received about the two bodies missing in the most treacherous part of the woods. He knew the swamp could take you in and you might never get out.

Murder, in his eyes, meant killing a large snake, or opossum, not human beings.

He was concerned about this affecting Amanda in a way that she may want to leave the farm.

He had no answers as of yet, but at some point he knew he would have to explain a few things.

He wandered……could his insane sister or his missing father have done this horrible thing?

"Where was Isabelle?"

"What has she been up to?"

"Who knows," he thought?

These were questions that would not be answered anytime soon.

And he thought, where was Slim?

I could never imagine him doing anything of that nature.

Daylight was drawing to a close and Thomas knew it would be a long night with all those things going on out there.

At that moment Amanda walked through the door.

"Everything looks great outside," she said.

"We planted everything and watered them well. I believe they will produce an abundance of beauty for us to enjoy."

"Slim told me, to tell you, that; he would tend to supper tonight, so don't worry. He went to clean up. He had more dirt on him than we had around the plants."

Thomas laughed softly.

The very thought of eating didn't seem appropriate.

Food did not compare to the two missing bodies. I suppose I could overlook this matter for this evening, she thought, but she could see that Thomas was not going to forget about what was happening.

At that moment Slim strolled in with the aroma of a cafeteria.

He had quickly put together a tasty meal to end their day.

"Time to eat," he said.

Nothing appealed to the taste buds of Thomas.

He seemed caught up in an unusual circumstance in which he had to deal with in his own way.

"Just not very hungry," replied Thomas.

"You must eat something," said Amanda.

"I know it smells great, but you can't live off of the aroma."

"I know," he answered.

"I will have a bite later on."

"I just want to sit here and think."

Concerned about Thomas, Amanda suddenly lost her appetite.

A nibble, a bite and supper was over.

Slims' efforts were for naught.

It didn't bother him because he knew Thomas was struggling with his own emotions inside and hoped that he would overcome the barrage of bad news.

"Well, I guess we won't be eating desert," joked Slim.

Amanda smiled at Thomas and winked at Slim.

"Maybe we can play some cards or something," she added.

"Not much on cards tonight," said Thomas.

"Think I'll just sit here for awhile."

Amanda tried to assure Thomas that everything was going to be all right.

Suddenly, she burst out loud the words to Amazing Grace.

Thomas and Slim were caught in an amazement trap.

They had no idea a beautiful person could have the voice of an angel.

"Now boys, I think I will go to my room and rearrange things."

"I need to get started on my writing, so I need to lay out an outline. I have a lot of thinking to do," she added.

She wandered over to Thomas and gave him a hug.

"Don't worry, money is the answer to everything sooner or later, and I have plenty to share."

"Good night, see ya'll in the morning," she added.

Sleep with one eye open," said Slim.

"I think I'll head out to the barn and call it a night also."

"I know he won't get much sleep tonight," said Slim.

Amanda went one way and Slim went another, leaving Thomas alone with his thoughts.

Amanda made it to her room with a large amount of concern weighing on her shoulders.

She really didn't know Thomas that well and was unsure he could handle the things dealt to him.

She wandered around in her room for a short time and unpacked a few boxes. It didn't compare to the room she had in the city world. Kinda small, kinda messy, and kinda run down, she thought. She believed with time, she could turn her room into a picture perfect place.

Speaking of time, it was getting late and she didn't want to make too much noise.

"SLAM."

Amanda yanked open her door so she could see what that was.

"I'm okay," said Thomas.

"I couldn't hold on to the cellar door and it shut too quickly. I think I'll stay down there for awhile. There is information from certain clues I've gathered and I must try to put this puzzle together."

"You can go back in your room," said Thomas.

"I'll see you in the morning."

Thomas shuffled his way down the stairway.

"Creak, crack, creak."

Nothing would stand in his way through his voyage of discovery.

A few steps forward he stumbled upon a large unlocked chest. Maybe some questions would soon become answers inside this old, dusty chest. A little junk stuff, a box of gum wrappers and an old rusty key.

To his surprise it contained nothing of any par value.

Three or four steps further into the cellar there was another large crate, covered with spider webs and two inches of dust. He removed the lid slowly and jumped back in fright. Hundreds of spiders crawled around the box. He slammed the lid and the eight leg freaks disappeared.

He remembered when his uncle would make spider juice and serve it to the children. I was one of those kids that believed in him. It took me several years to figure out that it was red Kool-aid.

A blue folder caught his eye. He removed it slowly and handled it carefully. It was old and the paper had turned a dark yellow color. I could see words through the stacks of stapled papers that I know I would be able to read.

At first, I thought I would wait until morning, but no, I must gather more information about my family, maybe information about Amanda. He rumbled through some medical papers, a birth certificate and an envelope of some old photos. Thomas didn't recognize anyone.

On the back of one photo was written, Mary I. McFarland. She was a young lady with beautiful dark hair. As I reviewed the hospital papers I began to shake. Whoever this Mary person was, she had been diagnosed with a severe case of schizophrenia. She was under lock down and received heavy doses of medication. None of the treatments performed on Mary were successful and she was held under the strictest security. Doctors indicated she was harmful to others.

The more Thomas read, the more he was amazed.

The next statement read; Mary I. McFarland, age 35, was born in Louisiana. She was intelligent, very wealthy and entered the mental facility, known as the Voo-Doo queen. At the age of 38, she escaped and has not been found.

Authorities could not rule out the possibility of a name change.

We know she only had a twin sister and had two children of her own, both girls that no one knows anything about, except they were taken away from her at a very young age.

Mary must be my grandmother, thought Thomas.

This is her old farmhouse and I'm a McFarland, so who is this unknown girl?

If he only knew some more of the answers.

There's got to be something else I'm not reading, he thought.

If she is a part of my family, then my mother, my sister and my genes say that I'm in that line of fire.

A scary feeling thinking I may become a schizophrenic someday!

Thomas closed the folder and gently set it down. There were several stacks of pages left to read.

I believe I've read enough for tonight, he thought. I'll take this with hope of gaining ground in the right direction. Amanda may have answers, once I figure out who she is.

Time was passing quickly and nearing 3 a.m.

Thomas slowly worked his way out of the cellar with numerous things on his mind.

He finally made it to his room thinking, tomorrow I will start the day preparing breakfast for my new cousin.

14

It would only be hours and the crow of the golden red rooster and the smell of bacon awakened Thomas.

Slim had prepared a smorgasbord of goodies.

Hot biscuits, fresh scrambled eggs, milk gravy, and hot coffee covered the breakfast table.

"What time is it," asked Thomas?

"About 6:30," answered Slim.

"I'm tired," said Thomas.

"I didn't get much sleep last night."

"Take your medication and let's eat a good breakfast, added Slim. I know it will make you feel better."

"By the way," where's Amanda?

"Maybe we should awaken her so she can have breakfast with us," said Slim.

"I'll go knock on her door," said Thomas.

Thomas gained a few steps forward and the outside door sprung open.

"Good morning," you guys."

"I had my five mile run and I'm energized and ready to start my day."

"Five miles," asked Slim?

"I get tired if we drive that far."

He laughed and invited her to breakfast.

On the other hand, Thomas was in a different mood.

Perhaps he didn't sleep enough, or……he gets major depressed at times and tends to be quite moody, maybe even irritable. He may switch back and forth without given anyone any notice.

He quickly snapped at Amanda in a disgruntled voice.

"Have you forgotten about those two missing bodies?"

"It's not a good idea to run around that early in the morning, all alone."

"I don't want to read about you in the newspaper," he added.

"It's okay," she answered.

"I can protect myself."

"I know judo, karate, kung fu and a few other Chinese words," as she laughed aloud.

She tried to joke about the situation hoping Thomas would feel at ease with her morning jogs.

Thinking to herself, she surely couldn't mention how she seen a glare of light or fire light deep into the woods.

She could feel someone watching and someone following her. She looked around and saw the shadow.

"Did you see anyone, or anything," asked Thomas?

"Just Isabelle, she replied. She was walking around in her yard. I tried to get her attention, but she was in some kind of zone. She was talking to someone, but no one was there. She walked up and down muttering something about a curse. Someone has been cursed, she said repeatedly. She was walking in circles. I went about my business," said Amanda.

"Not good," said Slim.

"She's into that voodoo stuff real heavy."

"She worries me sometimes. I think she goes into town and visits Ursula, the palm reader," replied Slim.

"She believes everything that crazy lady tells her."

"Does the sheriff want to know who killed those two hunters?"

"Ask Ursula," she knows.

"What about you Thomas, do you believe in this Ursula woman," asked Amanda?

Thomas put his head down for a moment.

Silence overcame the question being asked.

"I visited her once," he replied.

"Whatever she sees inside her crystal ball eventually becomes reality."

"She told me, she could see an entire family filled with insanity."

"She saw a man who seems to be a ghost."

"She talked about an old lady, gum wrappers and a syringe."

"I see a glow in the woods at night," she said.

"I see red......

"I see a road, and at the end of this road lies danger."

"I envision many bodies."

"Can't tell if it's a cemetery, or murders row."

"I see lots of money, lots of money, and danger lives on that road," she said.

She mumbled some sort of voodoo language.

At that point I knew she was off target, " said Thomas.

There was no money. I had a few dollars and my duck farming business was rather bleak.

"I had enough jive talk for that day," said Thomas.

"Still, you must be alert as you run pass the woods."

"Someone is watching you."

"I know because I can feel it."

"Thanks for the advice," she added.

They had a large breakfast and were ready to begin their day.

15

"There's a few things I would like to discuss with you," said Amanda. "I'll start from the beginning."

"I don't know much about my family. I was raised in a large city with wonderful people. I called them mom and dad and had an easy life. My parents gave me everything I wanted and needed. They treated me as their own child.

I was sent to a private school where I learned the rules of society. They excepted nothing but excellence.

I was raised in what some people would refer to as a mansion, but to the people on our block it was a normal house.

Every month I received a large check from....unknown!!! I never questioned that situation, just accepted what I thought was mine and went on about my normal living."

"Maybe that's something you need to look into," said Thomas.

"You know, where did those checks come from, who signed it?"

"There could be stocks and bonds or something," he added.

"This could be a missing link that needs investigating."

"Where do you start and what will be the results?"

"I never thought about it," she said.

"My life was so wonderful, I just believed the money was a part of it. I have plenty stocks and bonds. I don't need anyone else's."

"I planned on going to college and become a writer and then it happened."

"I was at the mall one day and….."

"Mall?"

"What's that," asked Slim?

"You mean you don't know what a mall is," she asked?

"Never heard of that around here," answered Thomas.

"Well, one day we will venture out into the world and you will see for yourselves."

"It's a large shopping area with anything and everything," she added.

"You mean, like a grocery store," asked Slim?

"Oh, no, it takes several hours to shop at a mall," she stated.

"Anyway, as I was saying….."

"I stopped in at the music store for my voice lessons and there he was, the man of my dreams, a knight in shining armor, my sugar for my tea.

"Our eyes met and we became friends. He always gave me that wink."

"Every time I went someplace I made an excuse to stop in and see him."

"His name is Billy Austin. He's a great looking guy with long blonde hair. He's a lead singer in a rock-n-roll band who travels from city to city. He works the night club scene and has his dreams. He plans on writing and recording someday. We dated a couple of times and we became engaged. He won't discuss marriage until he finishes touring and brings home the big pay check. I'm going to write him a letter and find out his schedule. If he comes to this area maybe I can arrange for him to visit for a few days."

"Would that be okay," she asked?

"Sure," said Thomas.

"Whatever you want, I want."

She continued to discuss her life with Thomas.

They talked for several hours with Thomas not saying very much. I suppose he was taking all this in.

Maybe he would get a clearer view of things if he knew every possible link to his family.

"Meow, meow."

At that moment, Daisy brushed up against Thomas' leg.

Her fur was soft, but her purr was loud.

"I think she's hungry," he said.

"I'll feed her and we can take a walk to Isabelles' house. I haven't seen her in a few days and I worry about her sometimes."

Amanda turned to Slim, "I'm going to get started in our flower gardens today. I'll pull a few weeds, till up some soil and plant an abundance of flowers. It will be a great day," she added.

"I'll help you," said Slim.

"I don't have anything special on my agenda today."

They stepped out onto the porch and Thomas noticed a cloud of dust approaching the farm.

"Sounds like a motorcycle," said Amanda.

"We don't know anyone who owns a motorcycle," said Thomas.

"Might be a delivery, or something like that," added Slim.

"We're not expecting anything," said Thomas.

"Could put a delay to your visit with Isabelle," said Amanda.

Within minutes!!!!

In front of our eyes sat two teenagers perched on a motorcycle.

They stopped at the edge of the ditch off the gravel road.

They were close to the mailbox so we assumed it was a delivery.

That thought soon disappeared as we noticed the actions of these two teens. They were laughing loudly, pointing fingers toward us, and trash talking.

"I see beer cans in their hands," said Amanda.

"This is not a good sign."

"Youth, alcohol, and motorcycles don't mix."

"Whatcha wanna do," asked Slim?

"Can I help you boys," asked Thomas?

The boys continued to point and laugh.

"I think the man asked you boys a question," announced Slim.

Slim was a giant man with a deep voice.

"Yeh," replied one teen.

"Ya'll those crazy people from that lunatic family."

"And, have you seen your sister around lately?"

"She escaped," you know.

"Oh, by the way, who's that insane old lady down the road?"

"She tried to warn us----

"Don't go down that road, you may never get back!!!"

"She's insane."

"She's nut's."

They continued to laugh aloud.

"She's usually right, said Slim."

In a more subtle approach, Amanda kindly asked the boys to remove themselves from the farm.

"This is not acceptable behavior and you shall be held accountable for your actions. We do not want any trouble, so go home and play video games or something," she stated.

"And who are you?"

"Little missy, prissy!!!

"Ha, ha, ha, ha, ha!!!!

Pointing at Thomas, the boys shouted. "How come you don't do much talking?"

"Are you crazy?"

"Are you deaf?"

"Are you dumb?"

"Hey, you boys seen that cemetery down the road," asked Thomas?

"Yeh," what of it, they smarted off!!!"

"Well, a lot of people who travel down this road end up there."

"I think you better beware," added Slim.

"Yeh, yeh, yeh."

"That's what that old goat------

"She's a bag lady," shouted one teen.

"Shut-up man," I was talking.

"Like I said, that's what that old lady wished upon us."

"It sounded like some strange language she was muttering."

"She repeated, over and over,"

"Cemetery Road, Cemetery Road, Cemetery Road."

"Someone has been cursed, someone has been cursed!!!!

"That lady is a real live weird-o."

"If I were you boys, I would leave out of here before dark," said Slim.

"You don't want to see the shadow."

"We're not scared and you're not making us leave. We will decide that ourselves."

"We're not afraid of the dark, you are," as they laughed aloud.

"Ha, ha, ha, ha,!!!!

"People in town say you sleep in your closet at night."

"Scardy cat---Scardy cat---Scardy cat."

"Anyway, we just wanted to get a good look at some real crazies."

"Okay," I think we'll be on our way now."

"See ya," wouldn't want to be ya!!!"

They laughed aloud as they rode off down the road.

It would only be minutes before the cloud of dust disappeared.

"There's some in every city," said Amanda.

"Humans acting like animals."

"I just don't get it, it's not Halloween yet," she said.

"Little punks," whispered Slim.

"They don't have anything better to do," added Thomas.

"They're gone now and probably won't be back."

"Maybe Isabelle put a voodoo spell on them," added Slim.

Hands in pocket, Thomas wandered around.

What else do we have to deal with, he thought?

"Did they imply that lunatic escapee could be a part of your family," asked Amanda?

"I'm afraid so," said Thomas.

"I don't want to talk about it right now. I'm ready to walk over to Isabelles' house. I need to clear my head."

"Want me to go with you," she asked?

"No, there are some questions I need to ask her. I'm afraid she won't talk to me if there is a stranger around."

"Okay," enjoy your walk.

"Slim and I are going to hang around the farm and tend to some repairs. I want to finish a few things around here, so I can go to the library. I have every intention on writing a book while I'm out here in the country. The sooner I start my research, the better," she added.

As Amanda turned around, she noticed Thomas walking down the road. His hands were held up high towards the sky. I'm not sure what he's up to, but maybe he was trying to reach someone in his own way.

She turned to Slim and asked, "what is this voodoo stuff you claim Isabelle may be involved with?"

"I would like NOT to go there," said Slim.

"If you need answers, you should see Ursula!!

"She will tell you what she sees."

"Towns people say she's loony, but, I think she knows."

"Knows what," asked Amanda?

"One day you will understand, but for now, NO MORE QUESTIONS!"

It would seem like hours as Amanda wondered around the yard trying to arrange flowers and organize a birdbath.

She pictured their yard looking as good as Isabelles' some day.

"It won't be long now and fall will be over," said Slim.

"We will have more problems in a few months and winter settles in."

"I don't know how Thomas will handle this years duck season. Most of our raised ducks will be slaughtered again by the hunters.

Thomas will feel pain where no pill will reach. It gets worse every year and that's a problem for Thomas' health. He can barely afford his medication and I know that causes him stress wondering how he will get by."

16

Meanwhile, Thomas continued his stroll towards Isabelles' house, mumbling and rambling on to himself.

Suddenly, a noise came from out of the woods.

Thomas looked up, and there it went, "The Shadow."

A few more steps and he realized someone was watching.

A calm feeling set in because he knew it's those two young boys, up to mischief and trying to put a scare in him.

As he continued forward, he noticed something in the ditch up ahead.

There it was, the teens motorcycle.

Two beer bottles, a couple of footprints and a gum wrapper were the only things he noticed in the area.

Oh, well, he thought, they're probably wondering around in the woods.

He proceeded on towards Isabelles' house ignoring all the sounds the woods had to offer.

To some it would seem a bit spooky, but for Thomas it was just *"Cemetery Road."*

He finally approached his destiny, but to no avail.

Isabelle was no where to be found.

A touch of weirdness suddenly crept over him.

Thomas noticed two skulls hanging in a large oak tree in Isabelles' front yard.

If it had any meaning, it could only be described as, creepy.

I guess I'll head back home, he thought.

There will be no answers today.

As he turned away, he noticed fresh tire prints in her yard, a two- wheeler, or possibly a motorcycle.

Pretty many ruts, he whispered.

I sure hope those boys didn't give Isabelle a hard time. They don't know who they're up against. She can move mountains.

A few more steps and he would be headed back towards the farmhouse.

The air seemed to be filled with echoes of fright and within moments, there was dead silence.

17

Meanwhile, Slim and Amanda were winding up their gardening wonders for the day.

They laughed, worked and they joked.

It was a fun day!!

"I think I'll go inside now, said Amanda. I need to repair my make-up table and hang my mirror."

"Need to look pretty for someone," asked Slim?

"Someday," she answered.

Amanda walked down the hall towards her room.

She never imagined having to re-arrange her living area to become comfortable.

Comfort was never a problem throughout her life.

Although she had tasks she wanted to tend to, deep in her mind there was great concern for Thomas.

She knew that the dollar bill could cure anything, but when it came to Thomas, he never imagined the meaning of anything more than a few dollars.

His duck farm barely made money, much less a profit.

At that moment, Slim shouted, "I see Thomas walking down the road headed this way."

"Wonder what he found out from Isabelle," he asked?

"I think we'll let him talk about it if he wants to."

"We can't put him under any more pressure than he's been through."

Amanda continued to move a few boxes around and set a couple of precious items in place.

She had a large collection of expensive perfume and needed a place to set her make-up.

City life was different from country living. She wore her Sunday best to go shopping, including high heels and make-up.

She wondered if she would ever need these items around the farm.

She could possibly save these moments for the day her boyfriend arrives.

Whispering, I always dress up when he comes around.

Maybe someday I'll get that chance. No one knows when he will drop in, but I'll be prepared. I'll dress to kill, she thought.

Suddenly the door sprung open and in walked Thomas.

His head was down and we could see a ton of weight on his shoulders. We weren't sure what to do.

Maybe we'll let him make the first move, they thought. We don't want to upset the apple cart.

Thomas slowly worked his way towards the kitchen, mumbling as he walked pass.

"Tea or coffee," asked Slim?

"Think I'll have a glass of milk," answered Thomas.

"Milk, something's not right," said Slim.

"You never drink milk."

"So, what did you find out," asked Amanda?

"Strange," replied Thomas.

"Isabelle was no where to be found."

"What's so strange about that," asked Slim?

"I think she had a run in with those two young boys."

"Her yard was a bit torn up and several flower beds were destroyed."

"Looked like motorcycle tire tracks to me and this is not good," said Thomas.

"I knew they were punks," shouted Slim.

"Well to top that off, I found their motorcycle in the ditch.

"They were no where to be found and that worries me," said Thomas.

"Did you see the shadow," asked Slim?

"Yes, and I'm afraid those two young boys seen it, also."

"Sure hope we don't read about them in the paper next week," replied Slim.

"Okay-----now ya'll are beginning to make me nervous," said Amanda.

"Why does everyone mysteriously turn up missing?"

"Maybe they're just roaming around in the woods," she added.

"It's getting dark," said Slim.

"What should we do?"

"You know the rules," said Thomas.

Slim poured him and Thomas a glass of cold milk.

He warmed a cup of milk for Amanda.

I think she'll need to relax after all this, he thought.

They sat around the table thinking what might be.

Thomas repeated again and again, "it's getting dark!!!!"

"I'm sure those two boys will turn up," said Amanda.

"Don't count on it," added Slim.

"No one escapes the dark."

"We need to see Ursula first thing in the morning," said Thomas, she knows.

"Ursula," shouted Amanda.

"Let's call the sheriff."

"Oh, they'll be here soon enough," said Slim.

"What's the deal," asked Amanda?

"I told you to write a book about "*Cemetery Road*," replied Slim.

It's starting to become more and more interesting," she thought aloud.

"We have to let it be," yelped Thomas.

"We have enough trouble around here without bringing back memories."

Thomas began to shake as he reached for his glass of milk.

"Crash."

To the floor the glass tumbled shattering into several pieces.

"Oh, no," said Thomas.

Slim tried to assure Thomas that everything was all right and he would clean up the mess.

"You just sit there and relax," added Slim.

"I need to see Ursula," moaned Thomas.

"Tomorrow," said Amanda.

"I may want to see her myself."

"She might tell me when my boyfriend will arrive."

"It's best you don't know things like that," replied Thomas.

"If she tells you things, you may regret it."

"Everything she sees, is not always good," said Thomas.

"Mostly bad," added Slim.

"Well, at what point do we decide to go to bed," she asked?

In a joking manner, Amanda stated, the worst that could happen would be two young boys trying to be a "Peeping Tom."

"I know they're not going to hang around the barn," said Slim.

"Can't really say," replied Thomas.

"I know what I witnessed down the road, and it wasn't good."

Thomas spilled out, "it's the same thing, two people missing."

"Where's Isabelle?"

"Where's my insane sister?"

"Where's my father?"

"Where's the two hunters?"

"Where's those two young boys?"

Thomas repeated again, "I need to see Ursula."

Slim knew that Thomas was having a difficult time dealing with things and was unsure how much more pressure he could handle.

Slim turned towards Amanda and whispered, "How do you know when his medication no longer works?."

"I'm not sure but, we will keep an eye on his behavior," she answered.

"We could sing, or play cards for a while to pass the time," she added.

"No thanks," said Thomas, I just want to be alone.

"That's fine, I'll go to my room," said Amanda.

"Is there anything I can do before we call it a night?"

"Right now my head is clogged with questions and filled with chaos."

"Think I'll go to bed in a while."

Amanda headed one way and Slim went another.

"Good night everyone, sweet dreams."

Amanda shut the door to her room.

She walked around for awhile.

Her hand on her chin was enough to know how she was concerned.

Concerned about what?

What's going on, she thought?

She knew it was getting late, so she forced herself to get ready for bed.

As she was dressing into her night clothing, a chill overcame her.

She felt someone watching, but once again, no evidence.

She powdered her body and dabbed herself with a bit of perfume. It was the only time she had for herself.

She turned out the lantern and climbed into bed.

As darkness filled the room it didn't take long for Amanda to become startled.

Noise in the attic, a shadow outside her window and a glare in the woods were only the beginning.

She immediately came up with an explanation for all three situations.

Thomas was in the attic.

Slim was the shadow outside her window and the glare in the woods has to be the two young boys camping out.

This explanation suddenly became question marks.

Amanda was not sure and was beginning to get a little frightened. I must not let Thomas see me this way, she thought.

All those nights of terror in the city and I was never this scared. With her eyes barely shut, suddenly there became a noise outside her window. Some one was pulling or scratching on the screen. I wanted to yell, but; I stayed silent.

I was shaking and for a moment I almost started to cry.

Suddenly-----

"Meow, meow."

"I was never so happy to see my cat," she thought.

As I approached the window and peered out, one of my questions was answered. Thomas was not in the attic. He was sitting out on the porch talking to himself. I didn't disturb him because he seemed to be in another world. I opened my window and there she was, my cat Daisy. I guess she was wandering around outside and got lost. She purred aloud as though she needed refuge. I picked her up and held her tightly. She was shaking and her beautiful fur was soaking wet. If a cat could talk she would tell me what's happening out there.

The wind roared and in the distance there was a glare in the night. Deep in my mind I was quite concerned about that glow I keep seeing deep in the woods. Once again I became frightened.

Someone was walking towards the window and my heart skipped a beat. To my surprise it would be Slim wandering around.

"Is everything okay," asked Slim?

"Yes," I replied," and shut my window.

I tried to be quite in case Thomas had fallen asleep.

Once again, he was nowhere to be found.

I could hear noises from the cellar, so I guess he's doing some research.

She walked to her bed thinking she could sure use a good nights sleep.

I haven't figured out how anyone sleeps around here, she thought.

I suppose I could ask Thomas if he has any sleeping pills!!! Ha, ha, ha!!

Things were okay for Amanda, but Slim found fresh footprints leading to the rear of the house.

I must keep this to myself, he thought.

As Amanda lay there she could smell perfume.

Her only thought would be she must have spilled some perfume. She worked her way towards the dresser and noticed several drops on the floor.

"Huh," she wondered.

Amanda was a bit concerned because one of her new unopened bottles was spilt.

Oh, well, just another mystery around here, she thought.

She had an over abundance of clothes and shoes. She made a special effort to purchase a red dress that was hanging in a store window. She knew it would be the right color and style for when her boyfriend arrives.

It was all worked out and she was waiting patiently for that day to get here.

It would only be hours before the next day would arrive and she didn't have much time for sleep.

Amanda could only hope that tomorrow would be better than today.

Each day brings another challenge and many unanswered questions.

18

It seemed like minutes and the sun was big and bright to begin the next day. A cool brisk breeze filled the air. The air was clean and the birds had plenty to sing aloud.

Amanda awoke with the morning sun dressed in her workout clothes.

As she headed out the door for her morning jog, she asked, "have you seen Daisy this morning?"

"No," added Thomas.

Amanda started towards the road with several things on her mind. She began her jog slowly down the road. She thought, while I'm running I will think. Maybe something will cross my mind in hopes of helping Thomas.

At that moment, something crossed her path as she ran past the cemetery. She was not prepared for that and it scared her so.

From out of the woods ran a large deer.

Within seconds it had jumped the fence and high tailed it through the woods.

It was suddenly gone.

I ran a little further and noticed Isabelle standing near the edge of the woods. It was very early in the morning and she was far from home.

As I neared I said, "good morning mam."

"Not so good," replied Isabelle.

"I didn't get any sleep last night."

"I keep hearing a cry in the dark.

"I can't figure it out, because no one is crazy enough to get stuck out here at night."

"It was a cry for help," she said.

"What about those two young boys," asked Amanda?

"What two boys," she asked boastfully?

"You know, those two boys on the motorcycle."

"We met them on the road yesterday and they were harassing us at all angles."

"They were mean, arrogant and probably drunk," said Amanda.

"Thomas told us, those two boys were in your yard and they tore it up pretty bad."

"No one is allowed in my yard."

"People come in my yard, don't necessarily get out."

"They're missing," said Amanda.

"How can something be missing, when it wasn't there in the first place," asked Isabelle?

Thomas told us, he found their motorcycle in the ditch and the boys were gone."

"They shouldn't mess around on "*Cemetery Road*," added Isabelle.

"Yes," but I'm sure those boys have a family and someone will be looking for them soon.

"Maybe we should call the sheriff," said Amanda.

"The sheriff is scared," shouted Isabelle.

"They know everything's a mystery out here."

"They're scared," said Isabelle.

Isabelle mumbled a few words, then disappeared into the woods.

Strange, very strange, thought Amanda.

Amanda continued on with her morning run hoping she could figure out, what's going on.

I don't even know these people, she thought.

Within a few hundred feet she noticed a medical bag near the side of the road.

There were tire tracks, but no evidence of any vehicles.

They looked rather small and she immediately thought motorcycle tires.

Amanda picked the bag up slowly and to her surprise, it was empty.

A few steps ahead, lay a syringe. She hesitated on touching it, but believed this could be some kind of evidence the sheriff may need. The more I gather, the more I get to write about. She picked it up slowly and set it into the bag. She put the bag near the ditch and was going to bring it home with her after her run.

As she continued forward, echoes of pain filled the air.

Every step taken may be your last. As she took those steps, someone was watching.

Amanda decided to make it a short run because something's just not right out here.

She turned around and noticed someone standing behind a tree at the edge of the woods.

"Hey Isabelle," is that you?

Thoughts of working my way towards this person ended quickly.

To her surprise, it was like a shadow----then it was gone.

It suddenly disappeared.

"Man, oh, man," I wonder what Ursula would say about this.

Amanda neared the area where she left the medical bag. Again, to her surprise, it was gone.

A gum wrapper lay on the ground in its place.

This is getting weird, thought Amanda.

There are way too many pieces scattered. If this is some sort of puzzle, it may take some time to put together.

Amanda realized, she should keep all these little pieces to herself.

I think I'll become a detective and try to figure this one out.

Do I become a writer, or an investigator?

With all my money I'll hire someone to figure this out.

She continued towards the farm with several questions on her mind.

As she neared the farm, Slim was standing on the porch.

"Morning," she said.

"Did you see Thomas," asked Slim?

"Not as of yet," she replied.

"I can't seem to find him."

"I called out his name, but he doesn't answer."

"I think the cool morning breeze is a reminder that's it's almost duck season. I know how he crawls into a shell during this time."

"I guess he's near the ponds. I noticed several flights of birds starting to migrate.

Second season is worst then the first, because you get more to your limit. I'll walk over and check near the ponds," said Slim.

"Is there anything I can do," she asked?

"No, we must take it one day at a time."

"I made breakfast, but I don't have much of an appetite," he replied.

Slim walked away slowly.

He couldn't imagine where Thomas might have gone. He continued to call out his name as he disappeared into the woods.

One things for sure, she thought, everybody just vanishes.

Amanda made her way through the front door that was barely hanging on its hinges. At any moment it could fall to the ground.

"We must put this on our repair list," she whispered.

She called out to Thomas, but no answer.

She walked into his room and opened the closet.

No---he was not asleep.

Could he have walked into town to see Ursula?

Is he visiting Isabelle?

Questions, questions, questions!!!!

Still, no answers.

As Amanda got closer to her room, she noticed the door was open and a gum wrapper on the floor. She always shuts her door to her room when she leaves.

She recalled, Thomas did not chew gum.

So—now what?

Amanda was determined to understand the meaning of all these clues and potential evidence laying around.

Suddenly, another kink would slam Amanda in a different direction.

To her surprise it was wide open and once again the aroma of perfume filled the air.

"Meow, meow."

There lay Daisy on a rug near the foot of the bed.

Meow, in a subtle way.

It was like she was trying to tell me something.

I roamed around my room for a second or two and then noticed my new bottle of Fifth Avenue perfume was missing.

Can't be, she thought. She looked all around couldn't find the bottle of perfume.

Amanda didn't care that it cost $700 dollars an ounce, she just wanted her perfume back.

In another strange twist, her closet door was slightly ajar.

Amanda worked her way towards the closet and realized her new red shoes were not where she had placed them, they were gone.

"Okay----

"Enough is enough"

"What's going on here?"

Amanda had a large stash of cash hidden in a wooden box on a shelf near her bed. The box and the cash were still there. Well, it's not money their after, she thought.

Amanda wasn't sure if she should mention any of this to Thomas.

She couldn't count on her fingers and toes all the strange happenings that occurred today.

Suddenly, Daisy was no longer in the room.

I need to talk to the sheriff, she thought.

It seemed like hours and no sign of Thomas or Slim. "Wonder where they could be?

She was starting to realize that there were more questions than answers.

19

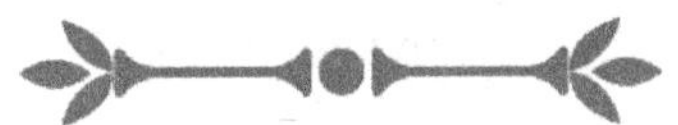

A cloud of dust appeared from down the road as someone was headed towards the farm. Within minutes, it was Albert, the milkman.

Amanda met him at the door with a smile.

"How are you doing today mam," asked Albert?

"I'm okay, I guess," said Amanda.

"I have your order ready, but I need to talk to Thomas."

Answering in a shaky voice, "I can't find Thomas nor Slim."

"Well, I will tell you so you can relay the message."

"There has been a report that two young boys have disappeared."

"Talk has it, they were headed for "Cemetery Road.""

"I know," she said.

"We saw them a couple of days ago and----vanish, they were gone."

"Every time I make a delivery I have bad news," said Albert.

"So, for a bit of good news, would you like to go out some time?"

"Maybe we could catch a movie or get a bite to eat."

"You don't know me, but I'm a trustworthy guy," said Albert.

"Well, I have a boyfriend, but I think he wouldn't mind an innocent outing. It would be another reason for townspeople to gossip," she added.

"Okay," replied Albert.

"Think about it for a few days and I'll get back with you."

Albert's face began to turn red as though he was a bit embarrassed.

He surely didn't expect such the answer he received.

"By the way," he asked, "have you seen Isabelle?"

"I stopped to make a delivery and she was nowhere around."

"Maybe she's with Thomas," said Amanda.

"Guess I'll be on my way. I have more deliveries and it's beginning to get dark and you know what that means," he added.

As he drove away slowly, Albert had a twinkle in his eyes. I believe it was love at first sight. He never had much positive feelings towards women, but in this case, he would swim across the ocean for this golden beauty.

Needless to say, Amanda made Albert's day much better.

As he drove a little further down the road, he spotted someone walking through the woods.

This person resembled a lady because she was wearing red shoes.

Within seconds---gone!!!!

He approached Isabelles' house and to his surprise, there was Thomas walking around in her yard.

Albert stopped, rolled down his window and asked, "where's Isabelle?"

"I don't know," snapped Thomas.

Albert waited for a few minutes noticing Thomas didn't have much to say to him.

He walked around the yard mumbling strange sayings.

"I been hanging around because I need to talk to her," said Thomas.

"Well, I have some bad news about two young boys that are missing," said Albert.

"What two boys," griped Thomas?

Albert became a little unsettled because he remembered Amanda telling him about two boys they met a couple days ago.

So why doesn't Thomas remember?

"Guess I'll be on my way, said Albert. I'll catch her delivery next time. I would leave a note, but I'm not going in that yard without her being around."

"Oh, by the way, added Albert, they still haven't found that crazy girl that's been missing from a mental hospital."

"Everyone in town has been on edge and many of the elders can't sleep at night."

"Some have talked to Ursula, because she knows."

"So, you should be careful out here all alone."

With a mysterious look in his eyes, Thomas whispered, "everyone has seen the shadow."

Albert drove away slowly, leaving Thomas alone with his thoughts.

20

Meanwhile, Slim arrived without Thomas.

"I searched and called out," he said. "I can't find him anywhere."

"I know he's getting low on medication, so I must find him."

"We'll take care of that medication problem," said Amanda.

"He'll complain because he doesn't take handouts easily."

"Maybe it's a handout if it's from the government or something, but, I'm family and I'll be there for him."

Suddenly, a loud noise came from the cellar.

"It's a good thing it's still daytime, or I might be a bit frightened," said Amanda.

"So, that's where Thomas has been."

"I didn't think to look in the cellar," added Slim.

Slim walked towards the cellar door and the noise grew louder.

He looked at Amanda and replied, "I'm not sure what that is."

He opened the door slowly and Daisy darted out, running down the hall towards Amanda's room.

"Wow," said Slim, "that's not Thomas."

"I think she must a gotten trapped down there," added Slim.

"Someone left the door open, but who," whispered Slim.

Thomas finally showed up at the farm from a long spooky walk down *"Cemetery Road."*

You could tell he was tired and had a worried mind.

"Glad to see you," said Slim. "I looked all over for you today," he added.

"I must of gotten lost or something," said Thomas.

"The day has passed and I still know nothing."

"I feel like someone is hurt or…."

Amanda spoke aloud, "I have found evidence."

"I didn't want to bring it up until I know more, but we must talk about this. I think we should tell the Sheriff."

"What's this evidence," asked Slim?

"Well, it's like everything else around here."

"It was there, then it was gone."

"I found tire tracks that led nowhere and a syringe lying near a medical bag that somehow vanished during my jog."

"And now, my red shoes and my Fifth Avenue perfume have disappeared."

"I better hang on to Daisy, or she might be next."

"We must think things through as clearly as possible," added Thomas.

"Let's not get the law involved at this moment."

"I think I'll visit Ursula," Amanda said jokingly.

Still, we know nothing about where Ursula came from or why she came here.

She came out of nowhere a couple of months ago and opened a run-down shop filled with voodoo dolls, skulls, snake venom and things we would never understand. I believe its Louisiana folklore. Her shop was located across the street from a funeral home.

She dressed poorly with gnarly hair that seemed never washed or cared for. Some thought she was a vagrant just looking for a hand out.

Incense burning inside her shop resembled the smell of death. There were only two colors of candles, the red ones were labeled blood candles and the white ones meant trouble. Red color was splattered on the window fronts making one believe it could be blood. A medical bag sat on the floor near the window. Her welcome sign hung upside down, while her open sign was backwards.

Many years ago a deep, cold cellar was hidden in a room in the back of the building. It is believed to have been abandoned and full of rats. A man-made dungeon even a strong mind person could never handle if placed there.

No one has witnessed this so-called room in many years but; it is believed to have been a wine cellar.

No one knows where she lives, where she sleeps or what she eats.

Some say she was a snake charmer whom has been bitten numerous times. Her veins were filled with poison from the Louisiana cottonmouth.

She had been injected with voodoo venom, which caused a dangerous form of insanity.

Surely this was town speculation and gossip, for no one had any idea.

She had little or no business and hardly seen around town.

People's minds became filled with eerie thoughts as they walked in front of her shop noticing the human like skeleton hanging in the window surrounded with cloves of garlic and dried snake heads.

Who was this woman they called Ursula?

The Sheriff's Department asked many questions about this strange person but, came up with blank.

Their main concern was that the two hunters and two boys are still missing. All of them are believed to have traveled to *"Cemetery Road."*

Townspeople asked the Sheriff, "please find out who this person is."

If "she knows" like everyone says, then she should be able to help solve this horrific problem.

"We will do this best we can with what we know so far, which isn't a whole lot at this moment," replied the Sheriff.

"We believe you guys pretend to be the law, cause we know you are scared," cried out an old man on the street corner.

There were many problems now at hand, and yes, the Sheriff's Department was scared.

They didn't have a clue to what was taking place and was a little nervous about finding out the truth.

"Let us not forget about the escaped patient is on the loose and they can't find her," someone cried out loud.

"We mustn't bring forth a panic to the town," announced the Sheriff.

"Please, let us do our job, and if you have any information, please come forth and help us clear this matter so the town will be at peace again," replied the Sheriff.

"There will be long frightful nights ahead of us."

"If we allow panic to settle in, it will only create more problems."

There would be greater concern because in two weeks it's "Halloween."

You can't shut down the whole town because of what has happened.

It's a tradition to venture down *"Cemetery Road"* on such a spooky night."

Surely there will be some that will disagree and lock their doors that night and stay inside.

On the other hand, some may try to sneak their way to experience the scare of a lifetime.

You must obey the rules.....don't be caught on *"Cemetery Road"* after dark.

Things were now scattered in several directions.

It would be a miracle if someone figured out the answers to all these problems.

It was now taking a toll on many and, still no answers.

21

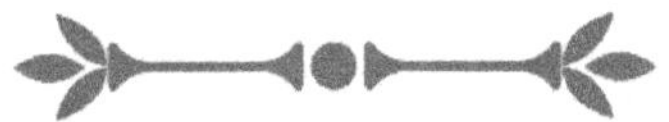

Night time had settled in and all seemed quite on the home front. Everyone kept to themselves and the evening would be at peace for once.

Amanda laid around in her room trying to add all the pieces together and writing them down in a journal she kept beside her bed.

The more she wrote, it more became evident, she had to write a book about her experiences. She had only been there a few weeks and all this has happened.

She still hasn't figured out how Thomas and she are related.

Daisy lay quietly on the rug next to her bed and every once in awhile you could here her purr….

"And then there was silence…."

Slim went out and slept in the barn that night with all sorts of things that were rumbling through his head.

He wasn't as calm as Amanda, and worried mainly about Thomas.

It would be a long night for Slim.

Could he continue to handle all the incidents that have occurred without falling apart?

"I sure hope this Amanda girl isn't bad luck," he whispered.

"And then there was silence…."

Thomas laid quietly in his room, on the floor in the dark closet…

"And then there was silence…."

The sound of an early morning rooster soon ended the night that awakened everyone.

Suddenly, a knock on the door drew their attention.

"Probably Isabelle," said Thomas.

"Hadn't seen her in a few days," replied Slim.

"I'll get the door," he added.

It wasn't Isabelle, but it was the Sheriff's Department with a few questions, looking for a few answers.

Slim paused for a moment, then asked, "can we help you, sir?"

There was no hesitation from the officer.

He quickly got to the point and said, "we have a serious problem that has everyone on the edge of their seats."

"We have an abundance of clues, but can't put this puzzle together. "Everything leads to "*Cemetery Road*," but still nothing of the missing people or their bodies."

"We are going to search every inch and find every clue."

"We started with the lady down the street, but she could not be found. There were four human-like skulls hanging from a tree branch in her front yard. Maybe she was getting ready to decorate for Halloween or something. All I know it sure felt eerie just knocking on her door."

"My deputy suggested we arrest her and end this ordeal."

"She sure seems to be a front runner just by looking around her yard."

"I must ask you a few questions and hope for some answers."

"Is there anything we should know about," asked the Sheriff?

"Did you say four skulls were hanging," asked Slim?

"First there were two, now four. Every time there's a body, there's a skull," whispered Slim.

"We know what we know," answered Thomas.

"Everything we see is nothing but a shadow," he added.

"We are all looking for the answers, but have missing eggs, footprints, a glow in the woods, expensive perfume, red shoes, and…..what's going on around here," he thought.

"What do you know about this escapee from the mental institution," asked the sheriff?

"Okay, okay, that's my lunatic sister." Are you satisfied now," yelped Thomas?

Slim noticed how Thomas was getting upset. He probably didn't take his medicine, and that could lead to greater problems.

"Our main concern is that it's Halloween in a few days. We can't watch every house and every street. We are aware there will be dare devils and try their luck in this area just for a hand full of candy. Some enjoy the thrill of it all, but are not aware of the danger they may encounter."

"We have two, possibly four bodies, a missing lunatic, a shadow, many clues, and more holidays are getting closer. Our hands will be full, but, we will cover every angle in this investigation," added the sheriff.

"Ask Ursula, she knows," added Slim.

"We have found nothing on this so called person and her voodoo known ways," replied the sheriff.

Suddenly, Amanda appeared from her early morning jog. She noticed the flashing lights from the officers car and became a bit shaken.

"What's going on," she asked?

"Just trying to gather some information," added the sheriff.

"By the way, did you see the old lady down the street," asked the sheriff?

"No, all I ever see is the shadow. This time it was wearing red shoes. I don't won't to think those were my shoes that are missing. It feels like someone's watching every step you take, but it's just a feeling. The woods are filled with echoes of fright. I was scared in the city, but I could see and understand what was happening there. I'm beginning to get a little nervous because of the things you can't see and what we don't understand around here," she added.

"Think I'll write a book about it," she replied.

"We'll leave on that note. We will search the cemetery for more evidence and hope we can dig up something," said the sheriff.

"Thanks for your time," and they headed down that dusty road.

They stopped a little ways down the road and parked near the edge of the woods. They could feel the sounds of silence. They got out of the car, not wanting to take that walk into the dark woods.

Townspeople were right about one thing; the officers were scared.

Several steps forward and getting deeper into the woods, a large raccoon with her babies ran out of the tall grass. Hissing at us and with teeth of a vampire, we slowly moved out of her path.

"Wow, that was a......

"It's okay, it's just an old coon," replied the sheriff.

"Don't be a scardy cat."

A few steps forward and suddenly, there it was, the cemetery no one wanted to enter. It was like some kind of curse to go near this place. Some sort of sacred ground or something.

Chills ran up and down their spine, as they looked at each other in fright.

"We must hope we don't see the shadow," replied the deputy jokingly.

It appeared no one had been there for years. It was poorly kept which made evidence harder to find. Tree branches lay atop the grave sites. Spanish moss from large oak trees covered most of the names. We then noticed a small path that led out of the cemetery. It seemed to have fresh prints that would slowly guide us to a run down campsite. We were approaching the edge of the swamp that was located next to the cemetery. Noises from the swamp were known to cause insanity for those whose minds weren't strong enough. The sound of a croaking bullfrog could be his death call if an alligator was near, or, a large cottonmouth might sink his fangs into the leg of the frog and not let go until the poison kills.

"Which one is more dangerous, the swamp, or the cemetery," asked the deputy?

As we walked the area we discovered four gum wrappers and a small syringe. It made no sense, but we kept these items as evidence. We walked and we walked, but still, four people missing and no bodies.

"Well, I suppose we should head on out. Maybe we can talk to that crazy lady on our way out. There's got to be somebody who knows something."

"Maybe we should ask Ursula," added the deputy.

"Everyone says she knows."

"We may not find what we're looking for, but we can say that we tried," replied the sheriff.

"What's that smell," asked the deputy?

"Smells like a rich perfume that only you read about in those glamour magazines," said the sheriff.

"Still doesn't make any sense," he added.

They walked on out trying to handle the silence of the woods and knowing they would have to explain to townspeople, they have nothing new to report.

Finally reaching their car, a person that resembled a lady stood near the edge of the woods. They were hoping to get close enough to ask her a few questions. In a blink of an eye she vanished into the woods. The smell of perfume again filled the air.

They headed back towards town and once again Isabelle was not at home. As he drove away slowly he looked into his rear view mirror and noticed someone crossing the road and running into the wooded area. Dark was setting in and they must get out before they see things that are not there.

22

All was quite back at the farm. Of course, everyone was a bit nervous, but that was to be expected.

It was not appropriate to bring up the subject of Halloween, but Amanda wanted to talk to Thomas about decorating the yard with scary ornaments and ghoulish items. It was only about ten days away and she wanted to get started.

Thomas wished each a goodnight and blurted out, "please don't take that morning jog," he asked of Amanda.

"I have numerous things on my mind and I don't want to worry about you," he added.

"We have things that needs to be done around the farm before winter sets in. We need firewood, we need supplies, we need…..

"We will start a new day tomorrow," she replied.

"Please don't worry and get some rest tonight. Slim and I will handle the most part."

Speaking of Slim, he was gone. No where in sight.

Amanda worked her way to her room and immediately jotted notes for her new book she was working on. She wrote for hours about her experiences she has had so for at a cousin's house she still did not know much about in relation to blood line. Everyone was asleep as far as she knew. Daisy purred, rolled over on her side and looked at Amanda. I think she wanted to tell me something about my book I was writing. Maybe some valuable information I should know.

I could hear the wind howling outside and the wooden shutters banging against the window. It was the beginning of a long noisy night… one night of silence, the next night of noise. It was an insane asylum in your own home. Outside, the blowing wind kept the sound of the crying tree owl unheard. It also kept the flame that glowed in the woods, a bright red color. Just another mystery one could write about in their book. Amanda slowly faded into a peaceful sleep. For a moment she had forgotten about all the unusual happenings she had been a part of.

23

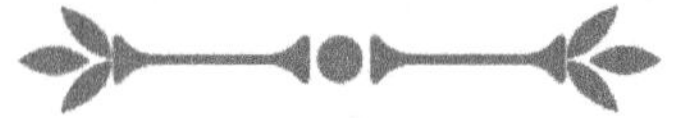

Daylight came about and Amanda slept a little longer than planned. It was too late to take her morning jog and coffee was cold on the stove. Thomas and Slim were off wandering around somewhere and Daisy was gone.

"Wow," she thought, "what's going on around here?"

A knock on the door brought worry to Amanda.

Who could that be, she thought?

She opened the door and there stood Albert the milkman.

"Good morning," mam.

"Hope I didn't wake you. I looked for Thomas but couldn't find anyone. It's the same everywhere I go, no one is home. Isabelle wasn't around, so I put her order on the front porch. It sure is spooky around her house. She must be getting ready for Halloween with all those skulls hanging from the tree limbs in her front yard. I thought I seen someone in her backyard, but I didn't recognize that person. She was there and then she was gone.

"Oh, by the way, maybe we should wait awhile before we go on our dinner date," added Albert.

"People talk dirty about "*Cemetery Road*" and blame those insane people who live there. They say things have been bad since you came to town. No one knows anything about you so they are a little concerned that you may be a part of this unsolved mystery. They're scared now and many are locking their doors and windows. Families are staying with families and friends are staying with friends. They know a killer is on the loose and wanders who will be next. The town is on alert and is looking for excuses to blame someone. Many young kids are riding around packing their guns and drinking alcohol hoping to get a piece of the action. Some innocent person could get seriously hurt," added Albert.

"The town is not the same," he said.

"Telephone lines are constantly lit with calls from concerned citizens about noises in the attic, barking dogs, and suspected prowlers in the night. Panic is beginning to spread. Fear has caused tremendous problems for our local officers. False alarms are wearing down the limited amount of officers when they could be somewhere else. They do not have the manpower to answer every call, like when someone hears a noise out by the barn, or an alley cat in the trash can. Women are asking to be escorted home and making sure no one is hiding inside their house.

"Yet, many are preparing for the thrills of Halloween."

"Fear and shock has swept through the town and horrifying stories are beginning to unfold," he added. Things are in shambles, but we must move forward."

Albert visited for a few moments, then sadly stated, "I must head on out. I have to finish my route in town. I will tell them you are a very nice person and I enjoy spending time with you. They will have to make that decision in trusting my word. I'm a man of my word and they know that."

Albert said his goodbye promising they would go on their lunch date.

"We have plenty of time to make other arrangements," he added.

As Albert drove away a cloud of dust filled the air. Amanda was left alone in her thoughts. She had no answers and plenty of questions. She talked a few kind words to Daisy and received a purr in response. Guess I'll plan a trip into town to purchase the decorations we need for our yard. It's going to be spooky, she thought.

Time passed slowly as she and Daisy had the day to themselves. Amanda had time to write in her journal and just lay back and chill. A cup of tea and a day of no stress were just what she needed. She made a list of items and drew a diagram of the yard layout she intended to decorate. She envisioned, spider webs, giant spiders, mummies, skulls, noise makers and other things she wanted to keep a secret. If someone was brave enough to step foot into this yard, then they deserve more than a bag of candy. As she thought for a moment, how many fools will try to step foot in Isabelles' yard.

A sudden slam of the door disrupted her thinking.

"It's just me," whispered Thomas.

"I was getting worried about you," answered Amanda.

"I've been walking around the ponds watching the ducks fly in. It's such a beautiful sight we should all witness. Soon, it will be massacre time and we will lose the war against the hunters. I wish they would see how I feel about this and maybe they'll understand," said Thomas.

"Where's Slim," he asked?

"I haven't seen him since last night," she added.

"Not good," he said.

"He's been gone for too long and that means he won't remember where he's been."

"Soon it will be dark and he must return, or…….."

Thomas walked in circles, mumbling some strange language, asking, "where is Slim?"

Amanda tried to change the subject discussing the upcoming holiday.

"Ghosts and costumes in a few days," she said.

"I'm real excited and can hardly wait. We had lots of fun in the city during this night of horror. I want to make it as scary as possible. I have lots of ideas and plenty of money. I'll get started in the morning."

The evening passed slowly with not much accomplished and Slim no where to be found. The sun was setting and the evening chill moved in.

"Think I'll put a couple of logs on the fire and jot a few more notes in my upcoming new thriller I'm writing," she replied.

"Guess I'll go to my room and think. I'm a little tired and probably I'll sleep in my closet tonight. It protects me from the noises outside and I don't have to see the shadow," he added.

"Where's Slim," he asked repeatedly?

Amanda assured Thomas that she would let him know if she heard from Slim and suggested he get a good night sleep.

Amanda stared into the fire with a blank mind. She pretended that Billy was there and she had been rescued from all this vicious canard that she never envisioned could be happening. That moment didn't last long enough because reality was reality. Her thoughts of Billy were like, the shadow, suddenly gone. Maybe she didn't want to know the truth about this family and the possible connections to these missing people and who's this Ursula woman.

Tomorrow, I will go into town for decorations and maybe I'll just pay her a visit, she thought. Why is everyone so frighten of this woman?

She fell asleep next to the fireplace and never witnessed the red glow in the dark back woods.

24

Morning seemed to come up in a hurry. It was a cloudy day and looked like rain. The season was changing and you could hear the call of wild geese as they flew above.

Soon, rice fields will home for millions of wild ducks and geese. Hunters will pay top dollar to get their chance for a live hunt. Many will use this as an excuse to get away from their family for a few days, while others will hunt to put food on someone's table. It is a way of life on the bayous and people from the outside world have excepted it. Some view this as a holiday.

Amanda and Thomas would go into town without Slim. He had not been seen in two days and that was another concern on the shoulders of Thomas.

As they passed Isabelles' house, she was seen walking around in her yard muttering to herself.

We stopped the car and Isabelle yelped, "where's Slim?"

"There's trouble in a few more days, you know, lots of trouble," she said. "It's going to be a horrible, spooky night filled with terror."

"Where's Slim," she asked again and again?

Within a flash she had disappeared to the rear of the house.

We entered town and everything was a bit on the quite side. You could fill the panic and fear that was all around. Townspeople pointed fingers and whispered gossip as we drove by. They knew what was gossip and that was it. Anything else was pure speculation.

There wasn't much spirit shown in getting the town decorated for Halloween. A skeleton here and a skeleton there about covered it, except;

Ursula had every possible element of fright one could imagine. This gave Amanda all the ideas she needed to decorate and scare the wits out of people.

They picked up a couple of items and headed back towards the farm. It was a quick ride but, they made the best of it.

It appeared the two most decorated yards were Ursula and Isabelle. We were about to be added to that list.

Amanda didn't waste any time getting her plan together. Suddenly a ghost or two hung from the front tree. A mummy sat in a chair on the porch. Blood dripped from the fangs of a vampire that lay near the steps. Spider webs were strewn across the yard with giant spiders crawling around the ditch waiting for their prey. Noises echoed through the trees that would frighten those in the insane asylum, not to mention the cemetery sits in the background.

"All we can do now is wait," said Amanda. It's just a couple more days."

"I think it will be lots of fun even if no one visits. We can scare our own selves," she laughed.

"I'm sure there will be the ones that can't resist the fright night on "*Cemetery Road*," he said.

"Kids will be kids," he added.

"I know it is not safe on this road and we must prepare for the worse," added Thomas.

"By the way," have you seen Slim?

"He may be to scared to come home if he sees all the costume creatures laying around," said Thomas.

"That's just not like him. He usually takes a walk around the ponds, but never goes for more than a day," he added.

"It's been two days now and still no sign of him. Think I'll take a walk to Isabelles' house and make sure there's not another skull hanging in the tree out front. Appears as though skulls hanging , means, missing people," he stated.

Amanda and Thomas managed to stretch themselves out for the next two days . They just lay around, not talking much, not eating much.

25

Today was the day spooky ones would come out and Amanda was not ready to let anything still her joy. She had everything she needed, including an abundance of rich dark chocolate candy and a roll of five dollar bills. She intended to put a smile on the faces behind the mask.

I think she meant well and her expectations were high, but remember this was "*Cemetery Road*" after dark.

Night came upon them very quick and she was ready for the first arrivals.

She didn't have to wait very long as she could hear giggling headed towards the front door.

There stood four young kids saying the magic words, "trick or treat, trick or treat, give me something good to eat."

It was pure excitement for Amanda, but not so for Thomas. She had a smile as big as Texas and felt like a kid again. She remembered herself being Cinderella in her days of Halloween costumes.

The kids said thanks and wowed to steal the skulls hanging from that old ladies tree down the street.

"She looked weird and she doesn't even have a costume," laughed the kids.

"Might ought to stay out of that old ladies yard," said Thomas.

"She doesn't play games with no one and you will never win anyway. She has the force of a magnet and will not let go," he said.

"She gave us that evil eye and no candy, replied one kid. She was talking in some stupid language, something about a curse, I think," they added.

"I don't know what was more spooky, her yard, or that old bag lady," they replied.

"I wouldn't eat her candy anyway," said one kid.

"She was there, then she was gone," said another.

"We seen a fire glowing in the woods near the cemetery and we decided we would check it out when we leave here. We're not scardy cats like people in town say you are," they added.

"Oh, by the way, nice yard lady. It didn't scare us a bit. Thanks for the treat and we'll see you around."

The kids shuffled on out yelping and howling until they were nowhere in sight. Echoes could be heard as they drifted further away.

"I sure hope they don't try anything stupid. They shouldn't go into the cemetery at night. It's not a place for young boys who think they are not afraid of the dark. Their tears of joy will soon become tears of sorrow," added Thomas. Thomas walked around mumbling strange sayings that only he understood. Sometimes he repeated himself and his worries were getting greater. Amanda was now witnessing odd behavior and hoped she could find a cure.

"Maybe those kids will find Slim," he replied.

"I think I remember him saying he was going to visit Ursula, because she knows," he added.

"We should ask Ursula," he whispered.

The fun was short lived for Amanda. The four young ones were the only candy kids that made their way to "*Cemetery Road.*" It was getting colder and all we could hope for was a safe return home to their family.

"We have a good bunch of chocolate left. We'll drop some off at the church so the kids can enjoy it," she added.

Thomas could care less about the candy situation. He believed there would be greater problems if something happened to those kids.

Meanwhile, these kids had no idea what they were going to receive on fright night. They're bags were filled with candy, while their minds was filled with stupidity. This would not be a good night for a treat.

As they approached the cemetery they tossed their bikes into the ditch. Each one brought a handful of candy on their little journey through the woods. It would be minutes before silence was upon them. They thought it would be possible to reach the glow that appeared in the dark woods, but fog was setting in. Each step taken was one more further away from their bikes. They pretended not to be scared, but took off their mask to see the dark a little clearer. A shadow appeared behind a large tree and suddenly was gone. The air was filled with the smell of Hollywood. A cold chill ran down their spine.

"Let's turn around, maybe this is a bad idea," said one boy.

"Don't be a scardy cat, the shadow's just that old lady trying to scare us. We'll teach her a thing or two," he added.

"Let's head for the swamp and try to identify all the different noises we hear."

Nothing but echoes of fright, once again filled the air.

26

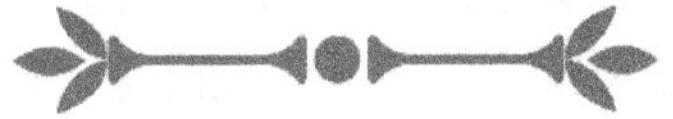

Night would soon turn into day and no breakfast on the table. This meant that Slim didn't return home from his lost journey. A few days have passed and he has not been seen.

Questions were mounting higher than ever for Amanda.

"Where's Slim?"

"Who's this Ursula woman?"

"Where's that lunatic escapee?"

"Who's behind the shadow?"

"Where's my red shoes and my Fifth Avenue perfume?"

Those thoughts would soon leave her mind because of a dust storm coming up the road. She could only imagine bad news approaching. It was just the mailman making his daily run.

Amanda ran out and intercepted the mail from Norman as though she was waiting for something. She was right, a letter from Billy had arrived. All her negative thoughts soon became positive. He was going to make a surprise visit and she was ready to see a familiar face. There wasn't a specific date, just in a couple of weeks or so he wrote.

"Where's Thomas," asked Norman?

"Not to sure, she said. Everyone seems to be missing," she added.

"I got some disturbing news to report and I should warn Thomas, said Norman. The town is in panic mode and no one knows anything. I don't know how much more they can handle and people can't sleep at night. Everyone's pointing fingers and speaking loudly about the situation, but the sheriff is scared and he won't do much about it. He tries to ease people's minds by telling them he has lots of evidence. It's evidence that leads nowhere. Try to explain to a family whose child is missing that you have no answers. They are getting worried as the list of missing ones continues to grow. Everyone wonders, who's next?"

"What's this about," asked Amanda?

"Sorry, to be the one who has to tell you the sad news, but.......

Amanda quickly interrupted, "are those kids all right," she asked?

"Not good news, they're missing and haven't been seen since late last night," he added.

"Parents think they were on *"Cemetery Road"* for an evening of trick or treat, but they never returned. Those kids should know better than to be out here after dark."

"They were here," she replied.

"Well, I think Isabelle believes its Halloween today. She has eight skulls hanging in her front tree."

"Looks sort of creepy," he added.

"Well, got to be moving along."

"Please, let Thomas know that I hope they get to the bottom of this real soon."

Amanda ran into the house bearing the bad news to Thomas, except he had slipped out the back and was gone. Amanda was left alone with her thoughts and was trying to find some kind of direction. If this was meant to drive her insane, it was surely adding undue stress she didn't need.

She jotted a few more notes on her tablet and was making progress on her project. A few words were now the start of her first manuscript. An incredible story was unfolding right before her eyes. She believed she could become a writer. It would be a great surprise to have a book written so she could share her experiences with Billy. Amanda then shared her good news with Daisy. A somber meow and a soft purr meant she understood what Amanda was talking about.

It was a boring day with no one around and Amanda felt a little worried about things. How was she going to explain to Billy all the strange happenings.

She wrote awhile, then stepped onto the front porch for a break. Squirrels were running around the oak tree having their fun. A pair of cottontail rabbits walked around the yard nibbling on the remainder of green grass. Ducks were landing in the ponds. Looking directly into the sun my mind began to melt by the cosmic rays which was reflected by the red wine colors in the water. Bullfrogs were croaking one last time before crawling into the mud for hibernation. The ponds were a second home for Thomas, about a mile from the farm house, sheltered by giant cypress trees. The ponds were as beautiful as the North Star shining over Bethlehem. Thomas would sneak away in the early morning to smell the clear smooth running water. It was quite peaceful and he made it a part of his life.

She could hear echoes of pain flowing through the morning air. Her mind spun around and around like that of a flying saucer.

For a moment, she thought about visiting Isabelle and possibly going to see Ursula.

"Maybe I should search for those kids," she thought.

At that moment Amanda could see Isabelle walking in the woods. Amanda yelled out loud in hopes Isabelle would respond, but she kept on walking as though she heard nothing.

I hope she finds Thomas, she thought. Someone has to do something. That would be all she would want to handle of the outside world and went back inside. A cup of coffee and hot biscuits fueled her body for breakfast. There were no more morning jogs and Amanda was adding a few pounds around the waist area. She wasn't concerned about the way Billy would feel with her added weight. I'm sure he'll love me just the same, she thought.

Her time alone was cut short. Thomas walked in the door as though he had seen a ghost. His pale face was white as cotton.

"What's the matter," asked Amanda?

"We have trouble," replied Thomas.

"I found their bikes lying in a ditch and I followed a candy trail that led to edge of the swamp. There were footprints, candy and gum wrappers, a syringe and the eerie sounds of the swamp. Very creepy feeling. I thought I saw Isabelle walking around, but I'm not positive."

"The air smelled like Hollywood," said Thomas. "There was no sign of Slim," he added. "There was no sign of any one," he said.

"I wonder how many skulls would be hanging from the tree now," asked Thomas?

"I can answer that," replied Amanda, "there are eight."

"I wish I could figure out what's the connection between the eight skulls and the eight missing people," he added.

"I think Isabelle knows a lot more than we think. Every time I call out her name she ignores me. It's like she's scared or something. Maybe someday I will get to know her better and find out her family roots," said Amanda.

"Probably should leave well enough alone. You might find out something you don't want to know," added Thomas.

Thomas walked away, hands in air, mumbling about some government conspiracy. "A black rainbow will form and the hail will fall," he shouted. He went to his room and shut the closet door.

"I suppose he'll spend another night in that dark, cold closet," thought Amanda.

Amanda could slowly see and feel the schizophrenia taking over the mind of Thomas. He had fallen in that trap of odd behavior.

Money was not the answer to solve these problems that have deteriorated the souls on *"Cemetery Road."*

She was beginning to wonder if her visit was real or just a story, a story that must be written, she thought.

27

Townspeople were hearing rumors about some guy with long blonde hair that got off the bus and was seen talking to Ursula, that voodoo woman, late in the evening. They say, she offered him a place to stay for the night, but he refused and he has not been seen since.

No one knows anything about this person who came into town and what was his business here. Everyone knows everyone and he was the new kid in town.

No one knows much about this Ursula lady either, and many are too frightened to find out.

One witness stated, he found a syringe and some folded gum wrappers at the end of the street. The air smelled pretty, he added.

He also said, he witnessed the guy leaving with this insane woman that resembles a bag lady who needs to comb her hair and take a bath. It appeared as though he was being forced to go with her.

Ursula had shattered the minds of these townspeople. They were lured into the web of unknown. She placed a spell on those who stared into her eyes too long.

She had plenty time to put a plan together while being locked away.

Little did they know, she had kidnapped the new kid in town. She tossed him onto a cot in this lost room many had forgotten about or didn't know about. She tied his hands to the post so he could not escape.

This new kid wouldn't be alone in this room that resembled a morgue. An older man lay helplessly in the corner. He hadn't eaten in days and couldn't remember his name at that moment.

In a low voice, he whispered, "please help me, it's been dark in here for days. My name is Slim and I'm scared of the dark so I sleep in my closet at night."

The new kid answered, "everything's okay and my name is Billy Austin."

He couldn't say much because he was weak from some kind of drug he received from Ursula. He could see black spots on the wall and the resemblance of a person laying on the floor. His arm was swollen and filled with pain from the injection he received from this unknown woman.

In a soft spoken voice, "I know of you and your fiancee' and my name is Slim, he repeated. I have been here for days captured by this insane woman. She has me chained like I'm some animal. I came to ask her a few questions and all I remember is she offered me a special tea she had conjured and I ended up in this room. She feeds me cat food once a day. She looks a little ruff today, but dressed like a million dollars yesterday. She smelled like a million dollars also. If I didn't know better, I would have to say she looked just like Amanda," added Slim.

"There was an enormous resemblance," he said.

"Do you know Amanda," asked Billy? She's my girlfriend and I tried to sneak into town and surprise her, but I'm trapped in this hell hole and don't know why," said Billy.

"We need to get out of here somehow," he added.

Not much more was said between the two because their energy levels were low. It was dark and cold and they didn't know what time it was, whether or not it was night or day.

The smell of perfume filled the air as they slowly drifted asleep. No one was aware what was on the other side of that concrete wall that separated the two rooms that Billy and Slim were locked away in.

An insulated room that had been turned into a mausoleum had eight new caskets leaning against the wall. A dressing room was never discovered by anyone and was a well kept secret. The back door led to a dark alley surrounded by tall weeds. It would take but a few hours to walk down this rat infested alley to *"Cemetery Road."* The air was filled with squeaking bats.

The piercing sounds of large crickets and croaking bullfrogs floated through the thin air.

"Ursula knows!!!!!"

28

Amanda had received news via the mailman that some new guy with long blonde hair came into town and has been missing for a few days."

"Rumor has it, he was last seen with that voodoo woman," he said.

"Very strange, I saw eight skulls and two large crosses in Isabelles' yard," said Norman.

"Not too sure what that means," he added.

Once again, it was bad news and tears were falling from her eyes. Nothing at this point was positive and she knew Thomas was not of any help.

She knew in her heart that this missing person was Billy. If she could talk to Isabelle maybe some answers could be reached.

What is the meaning of the two crosses. Amanda was smart enough to figure out what it meant.

It suddenly came to her….

Two crosses represented Slim and Billy and the eight skulls were……

She didn't want to think the worst but it was now reality and she must face it. No one was on her side now and she must do this alone. She no longer cared about family background and who's kin to who. Too many strange things had happened and it was time to move on. She knew she couldn't save the town and there troubles, but she had to save Billy.

There was not much that could be done because daylight was slipping away slowly and she can't take a chance after dark on *"Cemetery Road."*

She didn't have all the answers, but her story was getting closer and closer to an ending. She hoped the night wouldn't last long so she could start a new day. It seemed long because she woke up tired and sleepy. Her energy level was low and she moved slowly.

She called out to Daisy several times, but she didn't respond. She went out onto the porch and called for several minutes and Daisy was no where to be found.

This was not a very good start to Amanda's day. She had no idea where Thomas may be and now Daisy has wandered off. She could only wonder how Billy spent his night and what was her next move. It was like a chess game having to plan three steps ahead. First, I must find my way into town, she thought. I can run awhile, then walk awhile, and I will get there and rescue him. Amanda packed a small bag with her manuscript, red dress and red shoes. When I get to town I can stop at the café and change my clothes and visit Ursula. I must look pretty when I see Billy, she thought. Amanda headed down the road without looking back. There may be a chance she'll never return to the farm again. Thomas was at a point of such odd behavior that he probably won't remember who I was, she thought. There was nothing left behind that she couldn't replace later. She may never get to know Isabelle and never figure out who's family and who's not. Still, a flame burns deep into the woods and the shadow lurks amongst us as she walked down that dusty road.

The night was not so short for Billy and Slim as they were cold and hungry. They were allowed one bottle of water a day between the two, which was at arms reach from each other. They were injected every six hours with some sort of snake venom that slowed down the heartbeat and thoughts from their brain. Their vision was a blur and it was hard to focus on an object. They could hear, but couldn't see the full picture. They could smell, because Billy knew that Fifth-Avenue fragrance that filled the room upon occasion reminded him of Amanda. As he stared hopelessly into the stained ceiling he could hear the purr of a cat and suddenly, meow! meow! A beautiful long hair calico cat jumped into the lap of Billy as though she knew who he was. She purred and purred and they both appeared to be happy for the moment. The soft feline fur helped soothe the pain in the swollen arm of Billy from the constant injections.

Suddenly, the door sprung open to this hidden room and a beautiful lady wearing a bright red dress and red high heels walked in. She smelled like Hollywood and offered them some ice tea. Billy could see the resemblance of Amanda and wanted to believe it was her, but couldn't focus enough to make sure if it was her or not. She was kind and gentle and commented on Billy's long curly blonde hair. Slim sat in a corner asking, is that Amanda?"

"I can't stay very long, I have to visit my grandmother today," she replied. "I'll be back later to check on you and bring you food." Some hobo looking woman showed up several hours later. A large needle was forced into his veins and once again blood dripped down the arm of Billy. There was no food.

29

The Sheriff's Department was in total chaos. They were getting pulled in all directions, which have led to no where. Another missing person in town has everyone nervous and wanting answers. The most that had ever happened was a speeding ticket or some drunk walking around. Never anything of this magnitude, he thought. They sat in the corner of the old café drinking their morning coffee and having the usual pastry listening to town gossip. A morning whisper turned into a loud voice of opinions from many.

"I'm calling the FBI," shouted one concerned citizen.

"Let's get a warrant and bust down that voodoo ladies door, shouted another. I know she's hiding something. She looks like a bag lady, creepy."

The owner of the funeral home spoke out, "a lady dressed in red purchased eight gold trim caskets a few weeks ago. I never questioned what they were for, because she paid cash."

"Now, now, now, simmer down over there boys, we'll take care of it," answered the sheriff.

"Yeah, and what have ya'll done so far? Remember, ya'll are scardy cats, so go home and lock your doors," replied an angry old man.

"What about that new girl out on *Cemetery Road*," shouted another? I've seen her walking around town late at night with her pretty red dress, red shoes and her long black hair. She's stuck up, she doesn't talk to no one," he added.

"We'll keep an eye out," answered the sheriff.

The sheriff was a bit more concerned after learning about the eight caskets. He was starting to put the pieces together in his mind, not discussing it with anyone. Many strange things have happened since she arrived at that old farm on *"Cemetery Road."* It's beginning to make more sense, the perfume smell in the woods, she chews gum, and no one knows a thing about her background, he thought.

"Eight- missing bodies—eight caskets. Maybe I should bring this woman in and ask her a few questions."

30

Several hours have passed and Amanda was getting closer to town. She was a bit tired from her long walk but was determined to reach her destiny. She knew that within a few hours darkness would set in and she would be left alone in the small town.

"Where do I go, where will I sleep," she thought? She just wanted to talk to Ursula for possible answers finding her missing boyfriend. Amanda had extra time as she arrived in town. She walked slowly towards the café for a bite to eat. The town was quite at the moment with no one on the streets. The shop that Ursula owned was closed, so she entered the café, sat in the rear and placed her order. No one was there except her and the waitress.

"You look familiar," said the waitress.

"I know I've seen you somewhere before," she added.

"I'm visiting my cousin for awhile and don't get into town much," said Amanda. Not much more was said between the two. Amanda sat there waiting for the moment so she could change her clothes and walk across the street to visit Ursula. She wanted to dress to kill in case Ursula knew where Billy was. All she has to do is look into her crystal ball and then I'll know, she thought.

Amanda went into the restroom and put on her red dress and red shoes. She was a golden beauty. She slipped right out the door without the waitress noticing. The sun was setting and Amanda had nothing to do but walk up and down the sidewalk. The smell of Hollywood filled the air and no on was around.

Within minutes the sheriff pulled up along the sidewalk and rolled down his window and asked the lady a couple of questions.

"Where you headed young lady," he asked?

"Just waiting around to see Ursula," she said.

"Well, no one ever sees this Ursula woman, although some gossip about one day she looks like a bag lady and the next day she looks like you," he added.

"Young lady, I've put all the pieces together and I believe this so called Ursula woman has a split personality and that person is you. I also believe, that missing lunatic from the asylum is you, Darlene McFarland. What I say goes around here. You have fooled us for the last time and I will see that we put you back where you belong." Our town has been haunted by your insanity and has lived in fear. They shall worry no longer."

"My name is Amanda," please, "my name is Amanda," she said.

The sheriff put her into the patrol car and delivered her to Sunny Side Mental Institution.

She was placed in a straight jacket and hauled away by her long black hair. Tears rolled down her face as echoes of fear once again filled the halls.

She yelled out, "my name is Amanda."

Residents shouted out, "she's back."

"She will never escape again and one day she will tell the story of what happened out on *"Cemetery Road."*

Someday, someone will discover eight caskets and the bones of two humans and a cat.

Someday, someone will be called to *"Cemetery Road"* and discover a crazy lady living in the barn and a crazy man living in a run down farmhouse.

There will be a glow in the woods and a shadow at the beginning of the street.

TO BE CONTINUED